FRACTURED SERIES

BOOK ONE

INNER SANCTUM

JOHN MORRIS

Charlotte Greene

Dorset, England

Also by John Morris

Fractured Series
Inner Sanctum
Conspiracy Theory

Star Gazer Trilogy
The Gatekeeper and the Guardian
The Twelve Tribes
The Wrath of Gaia

Stand Alone Novels
Islamic State: England
Domicile

Printed in the United Kingdom (or country of purchase)

This is a work of fiction. Names, characters, places and incidents
are the product of the author's imaginations or are used
fictitiously. Any resemblance to actual persons living or dead is
entirely coincidental.

Published by Charlotte Greene, Dorset, England

Editor in Chief: Susan Dewey beeberrywoods.com/FiberEtc/

Cover: L. Fabry lfabry.com

Cover girl
Photography: african_fi (Belovodchenko Anton)
shutterstock.com/g/belovodchenko
Cover Girl: Alekseenko Oksana

Additional Graphics: Boris Junkovic
http://www.charlotte-greene.co.uk/Agents_BorisJunkovic.htm

Acknowledgements: Terry Dickerson, Monica San Nicolas

Dedicated to my wife, Siu Ying, & every woman who believes they
do not live in a man's world

Language: Fractured series, unlike all other work, is written in
American English.

Official author website: www.john-morris-author.com

ISBN Print: 978-1-910711-00-2
ISBN eBook: 978-1-910711-02-6

Table of Contents

Foreword

Who are you in your heart? Who will you become? Who will travel with you as your boon companion?

Shona Waverly is a fugitive from her mother's plans to sell her as a child sex slave. Searching for her own Inner Sanctum, she creates a family. Rosa becomes the mother of her heart, who teaches her the skills she needs to survive. Annaliese, a fellow seeker, is the sister who will fight at her side. Teves is their guardian. Through a change of identity, participation in the ROTC program, and the backlash of revenge, Shona and Annaliese have an opportunity to evaluate their roots and come to terms with the parents who should have guided them.

Inner Sanctum offers hope, help, and a model for those who struggle to raise themselves. Through confidential sharing, the girls form a formidable team, fighting against past and present injustices. Death, revenge, and remorse are just some of the milestones they encounter.

When Shona, now known as April, realizes that for her life to move on, she must confront her mother, Annaliese has words of advice. "April, you don't need a gun to go see your mother." But April is not so sure.

§

It is refreshing to read a book where the two main characters are strong female role models, and the main topic of conversation is not which boy they like. Although products of adversity, they never back down from any challenge, but rise to overcome everything the brutality life throws at them. It is notable that the supporting male characters never once take precedence; this remains the story of two adolescent girls from front to back cover.

Although categorized as Young Adult, Urban Fiction, the strength of the book, will appeal to a wide range of readers, both male and female.

The book flows seamlessly into Conspiracy Theory, the second book of the Fractured series. Book Two is a fast-paced mystery and espionage thriller, again featuring April and Annaliese as the main characters.

Prologue

Bill

"Do you think about sex *all* the time, Daddy?"

Bill looked up instantly at his precocious daughter, Shona, his life's work. Emotions whirled in conflict, alarm, rage, and concern. He blanched. All air and intelligence forsook him, as he gasped unusable atmosphere like a goldfish amid the shards of its shattered bowl. His sanity seeped away within the moment like water in the desert.

Thirteen-year old little girls should never ask fathers such questions. A new and uncertain look in her troubled eyes stifled his ostrich reflex. He looked at his baby, all senses aware. For the very first time he saw a young woman looking back at him.

His thoughts focused in that nanosecond parents have available to respond to life's impossible questions. Instinctively, he knew this was a defining moment for his only child, a moment of bravery that begged immediacy, and delicacy, to soothe the heart unsure of taboo's lines.

Knowing this, he did what any father would do, he scrambled for time. "Is this one of those *protean, protein,* or whatever you young girls label yourselves as these days, questions?"

She saw right through his imitation gruffness. Damn.

With what he hoped was bravado and not experience, she flippantly answered, "Oh Daddy, you are such a Crustic. The term is *Proteen*. It's a girl who's not legal, but all the men want her— what you would call jailbait, but a lot more aware." She sighed a bit wistfully and he started to relax. Then he heard her punch line. "It's going to be *forever* until I can legally have sex. You are very old, and know nothing about the world today, but I still love you, even if Mommy doesn't anymore."

He was losing control of the conversation fast. In all honesty, he was unsure of even being able to see the reins. Blessedly, by luck, fate, or happenstance, she finally let him out of the corner, right before a potential T.K.O. of his parenting confidence.

"Anyway," she rushed onwards, courage sapped by his obviously brilliant and deliberate ploy of saying nothing. "Tell me how often *you* think about sex, Daddy. *Girl Magazine* says it's every seven minutes for a man, and that's just gross. Yuck."

1

Inner Sanctum

As her father, Bill was more concerned about why she was asking the question, rather than his response. She was still a child, for God sakes! Her budding chest, and recent flirtatious manners on monthly visit days, made him question. His baby was growing up.

He had to answer. He grasped the nearest straw his mind focused upon, "Shona Waverly…" He stopped, because his girl was asking for the truth. He looked up and locked her eyes to his own, both of them sharing some almost intangible inner commune.

In that instant, Bill knew what to do. He rose and asked his daughter to fetch him a sheaf of paper and pencils. He went through to the kitchen and opened the refrigerator door, looking down at the large bottle of Celebration Ale he had placed there some years back, and reached for it knowing time had moved on. He flicked the top and took a long slug.

The kitchen table was set into the corner, as his bike took center stage of this room he hardly ever used. He threw the seat on the frame, and covered the dismantled engine with the gas tank, knowing Shona would take the only free chair. His bulk dwarfed the Super Glide chopper, to which he had planned to add a touring pack.

Bill gulped his first bottle of alcohol in eighteen months, or was it twenty since *She* left him? He could never remember dates, but he remembered every detail of catching her running around on him, the rows that followed, and how wronged he still felt. His ego had taken a severe knock, but he realized in that moment, the time had come to reassert his manliness—he would once more live his life the way he wanted to.

Morosely, he reached over to the drawer and pulled out a pack of cigarettes, and lit one. It was stale, but the heady rush was purifying, the first for three years. That was something else he had never been allowed to do when his ex-wife lived with him. Seated upon his Harley, ice-cold beer in one hand, and in the other a smoke, that was how a real man should feel living. He felt truly alive for the first time in years. It was time he left the past behind, and looked to the future. There was no avoiding that his future contained a daughter who was becoming an adult.

Bill's eyes strayed to the clutch left to dry over on the back of the stove. He had put that there just after Sally left him, planning a freedom trip, but life had become a black hole where *she* used to be. The crash of porcelain followed by a cut-off scream saw him rising from the saddle. Streams of curses followed, so he knew she was all right, and sat back down.

Shona stomped through moments later and used her arm to clear a space on the kitchen table, where she put down a ream of artist's paper and her father's sketching pack—the pencils and crayons he use when beginning a motorcycle drawing. Bill downed some beer as she approached him, and he took a draw of the cigarette as she positioned herself directly in front of him, straddling the front wheel with her legs.

"This thing!" She held up 'Rep', as he (or she, or it?), entwined its body around her arm in an effort to seek leverage.

Bill looked at the snake, "Your Mother made me buy that wretched thing for her on our second honeymoon. You remember, just after she joined that snake cult? It was virtually the only thing of hers, or mine, she did not take with her when she left."

The tension mounted as Shona fixed the snake with her eyes, watching it writhe against her hand. "I always hated this thing. It is repulsive. Mom says it is not poisonous, but I do not believe her. Tell me the truth?"

Bill replied at once, "It is venomous, and growing. All of this family of snakes are venomous. It is only poisonous if you were to eat it, you must remember the difference between the real meanings of these two words.

"It would probably not kill me, but I guess it could. Realize that I am a large man. You are what, one half my weight or less, although you are big for your age. It might kill you, or at least leave you hospitalized for days. It belongs to your mother, and I want it gone. It is a constant reminder of her. She refuses to take it, let me find it a good home, or release it into the wild. What am I supposed to do? I will tell you what I will do. It goes today, regardless of what she says. Bitch!"

He watched as Shona brought it to her face. Even from a few feet away, he saw the snake's infrared sensors flare. The tail rose vertically and quivered as if shaking the air. It was still too young to make much of a sound, a rattle.

In slow-motion horror, he watched as somehow, the neck extended, and the mouth opened, revealing long and prominent fangs of death. Shona was a match for it. She reacted instinctively while also staying out of range of the limited strike. That was, until she tried to throw it away, momentarily forgetting it was spiraled around her forearm. In that split-second, he knew she saw her mistake, continuing her arm reflex to bring the snakehead crashing into the cupboard she had fallen back against. Before her hand hit the wooden door, Bill saw the bite.

Shona reeled as the snake whipped free, coiled, and struck her ankle. Bill was already on his feet and reaching for the first thing that caught his eye. He ripped all six darts out of the board, and threw them in quick succession at the head of the disappearing reptile. The third dart caught it well in the neck, causing the serpent to coil once more and rear to face him. This time he heard the rattle as the loathsome creature came of age.

Bill grabbed a pry bar from by the door, and recklessly began hitting the snake with it. His first blow struck a fatal wound to the head, but he kept smashing the creature's skull until its head was a splattered pulp. His anger turned to fear, and he rushed to his daughter full of concern.

"Daddy, my finger is hot, but my ankle really hurts. Will I die?"

Bill replied unthinking, "No, you will live. Do what I say, and keep very still, relax, and keep calm. It's only a two-bit young Rattler, no threat to you, Angel."

Bill made her laugh, but remembered his Marine training, survival, and first aid skills. He knew this was extremely serious, but acted otherwise. He whirled Shona to the sink and washed the two wounds as best he could. Her ankle was already swelling. He picked her up and carried her through to the sofa, settling her down gently as he told her once more to relax.

Bill took a moment to stroke her moistening forehead, hiding his deepest concern, so as not to alarm her. He needed her as relaxed as could be. He rested her foot and hand on the floor, and told her to keep them lower than her heart at all times.

"I will Daddy."

Masking his growing disquiet, Bill looked down at the paired puncture wounds, so fresh and malignant on her left pinkie and ankle. He rushed to the junk drawer and threw out a bag of rubber bands, before finding the ace bandages. He took one and wrapped it first around her calf, several inches above the wound, and repeated with her forearm. The bandages were not too tight. He checked by trying to push one finger through against the tourniquet.

He was worried, but reasoned most rattlesnake bites were not fatal to humans. They were usually a defensive strike, and often no venom was released into the prey, as with her finger. Her ankle was obviously an attacking strike, but Bill thought it unlikely much venom had been injected. That was what he was hoping for. It was either that, or a mild reaction. He knew she needed immediate hospital treatment, so grabbed his keys and returned with two wet cloths that he tied loosely over the bites.

He was about to pick her up, when she keeled over and tried to vomit. She lost her balance and crashed to the floor, gasping for air as her vision began to blur. Her finger seemed OK, a slight bulge only, but her ankle was already discolored and continued to swell around the puncture wounds.

His only child was now in mortal danger. "Dammit! Damn her Godforsaken mother!"

He took a moment to slightly tighten both bandages, to slow the flow of blood, but not stop it completely—hoping against hope to stem the tide of venom coursing through her adolescent body. As soon as he was done, he took her in his arms. She felt limp and moist. She was wracked with pain.

With his life's treasure held securely in his arms, Bill ran past the quickest mode of transport he would have had, were it not in pieces. Instead, he made for the pickup truck, relieved it fired immediately. Shona was experiencing mild muscle spasms, and was finding it hard to breathe, both preludes to seizure. He floored the pickup and did not give a damn how fast he went, or if the cops spotted him—or if they could catch him.

This was life or death!

Once clear of local roads, he began to think clearly. The nearest clinic did not have the knowledge or expertise—sure, they had the drugs, but the staff were mainly illegals, anyway. Sure they had the kit, but could they use it? Would they understand the language he spoke, Texan American? The City Hospital was a long way away, and hours of traffic at that time of day in Los Angeles.

He almost missed the intersection as a voice wailed from the body, cast adrift on the bench seat behind him. The brakes squealed. He swerved to take the exit, and looked over at his

5

personal angel. He knew her life was within his hands, and his next actions. There was little time left to save her.

He heard her say, "Zzzzew." The sound came again, but slightly different as she fought for control of her muscles, "D-er oooz. Eh—eh, ze—ze dzoo." Even under duress she was trying to help save herself. Tires burned fresh rubber as all four wheels span, the large engine overly matched for them down the exit ramp.

The five-minute drive felt more like five-hours. He knew his Princess' life was slipping away with every second. There was a line of traffic waiting to enter the City Zoo. Bill picked his spot in the wooden ring fence, and shifting down, floored the accelerator.

Immediately he was peering through a mud-covered windshield, trying to avoid other people who were most definitely alive. Bill saw a running security guard, and veered in his direction. The startled man froze on the spot, and Bill missed him, just. He yelled through the opening window, his words a staccato; "Hospital. Snakebite. Rattler. Now!"

He nodded in the back. Abruptly, security came alive, realizing the significance. Shona was in shock, and starting to shake uncontrollably.

Bill opened the door and the guard jumped on the running board, pointing where to go, as he hung on for dear life. Security directed him by the quickest, though not the straightest route.

The clinic was small, grimy, and out of the way. Bill strode through with Shona clutched in his arms. The guard ran ahead and was already talking, as the receptionist picked up the phone. Two men in white coats appeared almost immediately. The senior checked Shona. With his daughter in his arms, Bill could barely keep up with, let alone comprehend, the instantaneous series of commands that issued from the physician's lips. He was distraught with worry.

They were led through a short rabbit warren to a treatment room. Inwardly Bill was seething, because he had bought that damned snake, for his ex-wife, and against his own wishes. He wondered how that had worked.

Bill laid his daughter down on the hard clinical bench, and dropped to his knees to ask forgiveness of her, and pray for her life.

Chapter 1 – A Snake in a Different Skin

Shona

Shona surfaced slightly and knew her father was close by. She felt his massive hands soothe her brow and wipe away the perspiration with a damp cloth. The dreams came unbidden once more, and were of nightmarish proportions. In them she battled massive, hideous, coiling monsters. She fell before them, engulfed. Yet rose above her inner demons and she knew she would live.

She opened her eyes, a lot more sane and focused than before. Her father was no longer with her, but in his place at her mother's side was another hideous, slithery monster. Creepo, Sicko, Rupert.

Her mother's latest boyfriend noticed her open eyes and rushed to her with ingratiating concern. However, once her mother finished talking on her cell, she did show some genuine sympathy for Shona.

Within a short time, her mother started berating Shona's father. Unnoticed by her, Creepo took every opportunity to stroke Shona's flesh out of pretended concern. She was repulsed, but could not move her body away from his touch. She felt trapped and hated him even more. His wandering eyes told her a different motivation.

Nurses arrived in a bustle of professional activity, having eventually come to realize that Shona was properly awake for the first time in days. They tried to usher Sally and her latest consort away. Mother decided they needed to leave for a pressing engagement.

Creepo smiled like a crocodile, and said as he leaned over to kiss Shona's lips in mock concern, (something she knew he had wanted to do since he first saw her), "We will come again tomorrow, Angel. I will come for you."

The grotesque kiss lasted too long and Shona tried to move her head away from his unwelcome invasion of her lips, her mouth, but it was useless. He tried to stick his tongue behind her teeth. Revo! Shona knew what he actually meant had to do with sex— adults cheating by using words with two meanings, and she wanted to be sick.

She thought Mother would protect her, but instead she whispered, "That's enough for now Rupert. We don't want these nice nurses noticing, now do we?"

7

Chapter 1

Shona caught the glint of victory in Creepo's eyes, before *Mommy Dearest* replaced him. She kissed her, offering her usual inanities, as if those would, could ever plaster over the cracks of what she had done to their once happy family. Mother flounced toward the door, yet stopped to preen herself before the mirror. That snake of a worthless male slithered beside her.

The nurses pulled the covers down to prepare her for a full examination. Creepo's eyes wandered over her thinly covered form, unobserved as always by everybody, except Shona. Surely, her mother knew what was going on, but she made no move to stop her boyfriend discreetly ogling her young daughter.

Shona watched as Sicko looked back at her. Not at her face though. His eyes fastened on her chest and groin, undressing her. Her boobies, as the boys at school called them, were not all that big, but her nipples were already quite large, and prominent through the thin hospital gown. Shona decided to kill him first, before she threw up all over his dead body.

Shona's body was still virtually paralyzed, her mind full of revulsion. This time instead of wanting to be sick at the thought of him taking her virginity, she wanted to act with a will to prevent him. Killing the creep would not be good enough. Shona wanted to hack him to pieces with a blunt cleaver, or better still, a rusty battle-axe. The thing she hadn't told her father, was that proteens understand this sick stuff, preteens do not.

The doctor was kind and gentle by comparison. He apologized to her in advance, but stated, "Shona, I have to make a full examination of your body, and no female doctor is available. The female nurse is here to reassure you."

He used the stethoscope, sliding it under her hospital gown as he checked out the girl's breathing. He used an occasional glance only, but looked her full in the eye most of the time as he did so.

From one side the nurse said, "Doctor, I am sure she smiled just then."

Shona was actually laughing inside her head. This most professional man was anything but a creep, quite the opposite in fact. The next day she could manage a whisper, and gathered that she was alive only because of her father's instincts.

The doctor explained, "Your life hung in the balance, and you are one exceedingly lucky young lady to still be alive. If you had not received treatment when you did, I doubt you would be alive today. A couple of minutes longer and it would have been too late."

The following morning she could croak a little bit more, and with help, managed to get to the bathroom. Those trips sapped her little supply of strength, but she was determined to succeed. Shona woke late in the afternoon when the nice nurse was waking her up for more injections and pills. "What about Father?" she asked.

She replied, "He's already been in today, with your mother. You poor thing, you don't remember."

Shona managed to retort, "That Sicko my mother is running around with has no right in our family. What about my 'real Daddy'? I know he was here at the beginning, I could feel his presence nearby."

The nurse apologized, "I'm sorry, but I don't know; I was only assigned to this ward yesterday."

Some minutes later, a more senior nurse, whom Shona did not like much, came to check on both of them. The nice nurse mentioned Shona's birth father, and Shona pleaded for information.

The senior nurse's haughty face turned grim as she thought for a second. Within a moment she lightened with her false smile and beamed, "Ah. Bill Waverley. Yes, he came with you when you arrived here at City General from the Zoo. I thought that an odd place to take you, but apparently it was what saved your life."

She turned away, as if she had assuaged Shona's question. But the nurse had dismissed it, not answered it. Shona shouted as loudly as possible, "What has happened to him? Why hasn't Daddy been to see me?"

Not used to being spoken down to, especially by a proteen, the head nurse whirled as anger crossed her face, before the reptilian smile reappeared, "Child, your *birth father* stayed until late the next morning after he brought you here. It was against hospital regulations, but, well, let's say he is a *very* large man and he was extremely concerned about you. He was also no trouble, otherwise, we would have called a full security detail to remove him.

"However, Sister said that as long as he was good as gold, it was better for all if he stayed. She seemed to think he was devoted to you, although I cannot imagine why."

Shona thought, *What a sanctimonious cow.*

Chapter 1

She was determined to get an answer from the smarmy bitch, so she pressed again, "Thank you nurse, but where is he, why has he not been here since?"

The head nurse stood and stared at Shona for a full ten seconds, before answering in an offhand, condescending, and concluding manner, "My dear, I am sorry, but I do not know. I am sure you will see him as soon as possible. Now, Nurse, please administer the sedative."

Shona knew this did not answer the question she had asked, but as the drugs took control of her body and mind, it remained all she was left with, for today.

By mid-morning of the next day, Shona was starting to feel well again. Her strength was returning, and so was her determination. She tried to call her Daddy several times, but there was never any reply. She began to worry something serious had happened to him. She knew he would have been at her bedside if he were a free man.

Mother and *IT* arrived for their daily visit; "Some of your friends at school posted cards through the door, I thought they might look better here, than cluttering up our home. Rupert, be a darling and place them appropriately."

"Huh? You stopped every friend I ever had coming to *our* home, mother. I don't have any friends, because of you!"

A row erupted, but afterwards, when they made to leave, Shona had managed to stop Creepo from kissing her lips again, by twisting his wrist against the joint, as she had learned in Kung Fu. She held him so he had to move his head away from her own, but as she relaxed her grip, he wriggled in to kiss her wrist. She was still too immobile to react quickly enough, and endured as he surreptitiously licked the back of her hand, until she punched him.

She felt utter revulsion, and later imagined all sorts of diabolical things that she would one day do to him. Their battle lines were being drawn on her recovery bed. On one side lay Shona's virginity, on the other, Creepo's life and her self-respect. It was coming down to that.

"Why hasn't Daddy come to see me?"

Mother's anger flared, as Shona knew it would, and she replied with venom. "That useless male. I don't know why I ever married him. He insisted on buying that snake, even though I did not want it. God knows why he kept it so long. I guess they were soul mates."

Shona shouted back, "We both know that is a lie, Mother. You made him buy the snake. I remember you gloating about what a laugh it was to try and control him that way, force him to do something he did not want to do."

Her mother's face turned red, and she slapped her daughter hard on the cheek. She stood back to admire her handiwork, "We are leaving now. This worthless slut is as bad as her father. Come on Rupert. I have better things to do than waste my time here."

Rupert was taken aback, and Shona was stunned, not by the blow, but by her mother's words and abrupt departure. She was slow to realize Creepo was about to kiss her lips, when she instinctively reacted to his unwelcome advance. Her strength was growing, and she managed to punch him on the jaw. He reeled away, but her mother replaced him and swung to hit her again, harder. Shona parried the blow easily, almost breaking her mother's arm in the process.

As her mother backed away, Shona spat cruel words of harsh truth, "Mother, you do know he wants to have sex with me, don't you?"

Her mother never looked at Shona again. She turned and flounced away, speaking only to her boyfriend, "Rupert, come. She is clearly old enough, it is time to put our plan into motion."

Shona was left alone to think. There was little else to do— what plan? She did wonder if her mother made her father keep the rattler in the hope he would be bitten by it, and die. She knew her mother still had insurance on their lives. The more she thought about it, the more it made sense.

Shona changed from being a proteen to an adult in those few hours. With no distractions, she observed what had actually happened within her mind, what had been said, versus what had been done, the lies and half-truths. By focusing her excellent memory on the senior nurse, Shona was able to recall the answers to her questions—they conflicted. She had tried several times, and had still not received a satisfactory reply.

Shona had been distracted by this, but had moved on to thinking about where her father could be, when a scattered thought came to her. She spoke it out loud for clarity, "Adults only ever tell you enough information to stem your inquisitiveness or staunch your understanding. They never, ever, tell you the whole truth—and that is the only thing that is important."

She had been thinking similar things for several years, but now she had proof, and was now wise to their games. She determined to use this knowledge against them, since often what adults did not say was much more important than what they did say. She now knew mother and Sicko had a plan that involved her, and she determined to find out what it was.

The next day passed even slower, until her father turned up. Shona was delighted to see him, and they talked for hours. She loved being with him, and could see he was healed. Bill's old personality had reasserted itself. He confirmed this by saying, "I have missed you so much, and wanted to be here with you, but something came up."

"What happened Daddy?" Shona asked, full of concern.

Bill smiled and said, "Nothing much, but it was a close call. I went back to the Zoo on Monday morning, and offered to fix the fence, pay damages, to make amends as best I could. The manager was some young kid who wanted to play it all by the book. I talked him out of instructing their lawyer to sue me, but he insisted the cops be called.

"I waited for them to arrive, and they arrested me for property damage. I was interrogated and they wanted to press charges, despite my defense of saving your life. I even got a supporting statement from one of the doctors who treated you.

"I was held in a cell overnight, but did get a message out to an old buddy who knew me from the Marine Corps. I knew he now worked for the cops, and he dropped by to see me the next morning. He told me to lawyer-up, and gave a character statement in support of my defense."

Shona replied, "Daddy, this is so unfair. I can't believe they put you through all this. I hope they let you go right away?"

Bill chuckled and shook his head. He continued speaking, but now there was a sparkle in his eyes, "They questioned me twice more that day, and again the next morning. My lawyer told me to say nothing, as all they were trying to do was get me to admit my guilt.

"I did get news about you, and was so relieved when I heard that your condition had stabilized. I would be lost without you."

Shona held him tight as they hugged, but Bill gathered himself moments later, and finished the tale.

"They dropped all charges but still wanted to give me a formal warning. I tried to see you but you have been sedated until today. I collected the pick-up and paid for the damages, then went home and fixed the bike. You know, she fired first time."

Doctor's rounds interrupted them. Bill refused to leave when the doctor arrived, and got a full breakdown of his daughter's condition and recuperation. Shona learned she was almost healed, and would be released in a day or two. They hugged in happiness, and Bill kissed her on the forehead.

When the medics left, Bill asked her, "Hon, do you mind if I head-off for my freedom trip. The bike's all fixed up now, and I can't wait to take you for a spin. I know you always loved the rush—maybe I'll let you take her for a ride on a quiet road somewhere..."

His talk moved on to his planned journey. "I have an old buddy, John, to see before I leave. You know him. I'll leave a burner phone for you at his place. I don't need everybody tracking where I'm going. If you ever go off the grid, remember to always pay cash and use burner cells..."

A nurse came in to check and sedate Shona. Bill asked her for more time, and was benevolently forceful enough for the nurse to go away. He proceeded to tell his daughter about the life of The Outlaw, and she knew it was his dream. Her father was taking the moment to make it come true.

Bill finished by saying, "Hon, I'm gonna take one more ride on ma luck, put the wheels on the road, and no looking back—except for you.

"I love you, never forget that."

The head nurse came in just then and was firm. "Mr. Waverley, if you please. Your daughter must be sedated, and your time is up. Please leave now, otherwise, we will not be able to release her tomorrow. Good day, Sir."

Bill stood and bent towards his daughter, looking deep into her eyes. He kissed her briefly on the lips, and Shona welcomed it. It was a fatherly kiss, not one from a pervert.

She wanted to tell him about Rupert, and mother, but knew he would cancel his freedom trip, and probably kill both of them instead. She knew about his war days in Nicaragua, when he had killed many Sandinista guerillas.

Bill pulled back and whispered in her ear, "I'm gonna be off the grid for a while. I'll call you from a burner cell in a few days."

The nurse tried to bully him out of the way, but he took his time and casually picked up his leather Hells Angels jacket from the chair. Walking to the door he turned back, and as was his way, clenched his fist, before extending his arm, index finger, and thumb, pointing at Shona, and said, "You."

Shona made the same gesture, and said "You" back. She loved him, he was so much of a man.

Chapter 2 – "Gather ye rosebuds while ye may"

Shona knew before she walked into her mother's latest house, it was no longer her home. How could it be? The rows began in the car, and they continued arguing at the house. Shona asked Sally repeatedly why she had left Bill, until her mother lost her temper and hit her. Her mother ordered her never to mention her father's name again, and told her to watch TV with her (fake) new father. Gross. *IT* and Shona were watching Hannah Montana and he was trying to give her clues as how to become another Miley Cyrus. Imbecile—who'd want to, except for perverts like him.

Shona corrected him, "In this ancient teenage angst sitcom, she plays the part of Miley Ray Stewart. However, her real name was Destiny Hope Cyrus…"

She was so engrossed in correcting the plebe that she waved her hands around in exaggeration, and that was when he tried to grab them, contriving to feel her right boobie as he did so. Shona shot up and kicked him hard. Mother came in to shout at her, but she ignored the woman and stomped up to her room, locking the door and bolting it behind her. She was fuming at being so stupid.

Later, tears came as she began to realize how hard it was to be a proteen in a world full of corrupt and unscrupulous adults.

"I wish my father were here." Shona knew she said it aloud and repeated it over, and over again, a mantra to keep her sane, if only for the night.

Much later, a slight noise distracted her, and she watched with mounting horror as the doorknob turned several times. Shona knew she was being hunted when the slight scrape of a key entered the lock. She ran to the door still overflowing with emotions and shouted, "*Fuck—off—pervert!* I've bolted this door from the inside to stop *YOU* from getting in."

His attempt appeared to flounder, and eventually Shona managed to sleep, late at night.

The next night after dinner, they were watching TV, although now she curled up in a blanket, despite the hot summer evening, to prevent Sicko from getting anywhere near her. She knew time was wasting, and went up to her room to study, but her mind would not focus. She kept wondering what they were planning for her.

Chapter 2

Needing to find out, she crept downstairs, avoiding the creaks, and listened from the kitchen. The room had three doors: one to the hall, one to the living room, and a third to the mudroom and back door. They were watching TV and not speaking.

Shona was about to return to her room, when the telephone rang. She only heard her mother's side of the conversation, but it was enough to fill her with dread. "Hello ... yes, when will you come for her? ... Friday will be fine. I will make sure she is prepared for you. What time suits you best? ... Nine it is then, and we exchange the money first, before I hand her over. ... Yes, she is still a virgin, I had her hymen checked just a few days ago. ... A bonus, thank you, that is so kind."

Mother put down the phone and said to Rupert, "They accepted the deal. Fifteen thousand dollars for the first time, and thirty percent of whatever they charge others afterwards. At last she will be doing something useful and earning us easy money."

Shona's mind shattered. Surely, her own mother could not be talking about selling her virginity, and trafficking her as an underage sex slave. Mothers don't do that.

Her mother's next words intruded into Shona's thoughts, "Rupert, be a love and get the wine out of the refrigerator to celebrate our good fortune."

Shona bolted for her bedroom, her mind screaming. Surely, this could not be happening to her? She felt mad, devastated. She needed to lash out, and the only one she could hurt was herself.

She wanted to cut herself and let out whatever evil thing inside her was causing her mother to punish her in this way. She took a razor to her bedroom, sat down at her vanity, composed herself, and drew the blade across her wrist. The wound stung, but not as much as the pain in her heart. She went to make a second, deeper cut, but stopped. She remembered how some girls at school had done it, near the elbow. It looked cool—until you looked into their defeated eyes. Shona would never be defeated. She looked down at her wrist and did not think the mark looked cool on her. It was a sign of weakness, a cry for help, an admission of defeat. She would be strong and help herself.

The mark was still there the next day, Wednesday, but it would soon heal. Mother never noticed, although it was obvious. Creepo tried to lick it. Shona jabbed her fingers in his eyes and got away.

She rushed up to her room and looked down at the razor blade. "Cutting, huh? Why bother hurting myself, when I should be using my razor to slit Sicko's throat?"

She spent several hours in blissful dignity, imagining all the ways and situations that she could easily accomplish that small thing. Shona wanted him to beg for his life, just before she willfully murdered him.

The changes came quickly after that enlightening night. Shona stopped wearing jelly bracelets, telling everyone at school the next day, they were old and dated. Her real reason was that she understood that they threatened in real life, an eternally childish existence of sexual exploitation.

Instead, she suffered in silence, spending more time the next evening checking where Creepo's hands were, than watching TV.

IT, That Creepo, Sicko, was in her house, and very much against her wishes. *Mommy Dearest* said she loved him, and that he was the best thing for their future and prosperity. Shona wanted to kill him. She hated her mother. Shona was so absorbed with thoughts about her current predicament and memories of better times, that she went for an evening shower to wash away the macabre recollections.

Shona was under the monsoon and well into her head with eyes closed. She had been caressing her unnaturally hurtful and flowering nipples with a soft bar of gentling rose-petal soap, trying to determine what the new and complicated sensations meant for her future. Unexpectedly there was something happening below— in a place she never realized existed before. She said to herself, "This is interesting. Nice."

Her hand slowly circled the soap down her body, curious yet leisurely, seeking the source of this new sensation. Very nice.

Absorbed in this life-changing moment, her own thoughts and bodily reactions, she was totally unprepared for the click and perceived flash. She knew at once she had forgotten to bolt the bathroom door. In total shock and realization she came aware, her eyes flying open at the grossly unwanted invasion of her personal privacy, only to be blurred by the cascading water. She was blind. Creepo's lips tried to fasten on her nipple as he groped her, and the sensations deep below increased dramatically. *Damn him!*

She reacted instinctively, the soap allowing her to slip from his grasp. She turned the attack on him, using Kung Fu skills to batter

17

any part of him she could hit with force. He fell back as Shona continued her assault, her eyes clearing, and her aim becoming true. She knew she was hurting him badly, and he deserved each, and every strike.

Shona would probably have killed him, had she not heard her mother charging up the stairs. She ran to her bedroom and bolted the door, securing it with a chair wedged below the handle.

Her body was alive with action, but she calmed herself to listen at the keyhole, "Rupert, I thought we had a deal. You are not allowed to take her virginity. It is worth too much money. Do you understand? You can take her later."

So there it was. The Mother from Hell had confirmed her existence. Shona, her only child was to be her mother's victim, and she didn't care about Shona at all. She only cared about the money her daughter's young body could make for her. Something died within. She flung herself on her bed and cried. A thunderstorm raged outside, and matched her mood perfectly; the thunder the deep chasm in her heart where love once dwelt, and the downpour that followed, her tears.

Mother banged on Shona's door and threatened her with many fates worse than death. She was grounded forever. They pounded the door, and although the frame started to give, the chair propped under the handle stopped them. Shona had to get out of there.

She started to pack essentials, before she realized that what she was packing was useless. It was kid stuff and she couldn't be a kid any longer. Shona imagined Bonnie and Clyde. What would she throw in a bag? And Katniss Everdeen? She added the book about her, one of her favorites. What was essential to survival? She opened her suitcase and knew that she had it all wrong. They had stopped banging on the door and had gone downstairs. At last, she had some private time to think.

She emptied her school backpack onto the floor, intending to fill it with new essentials for survival in the wild. She picked up the empty sack, and realized the bright pink with ice blue stripes on searing white background would stand out a mile everywhere she went. This was her only backpack, and the only one in the house. She had to use it. She swapped and changed things over, knowing she would be wearing a bull's eye for identification. She would change it as soon as she could.

Shona placed the school books and homework to one side, but packed her personal notebook, plus a few pencils and added her artwork from the secret drawer—something only her father knew about. Apart from a few knick-knacks, this represented the sum total of who she was as an individual. It seemed to her, it did not amount to much of anything.

"I'm gonna be somebody!" she shouted, punching her fist in the air, before threatening the mirror.

Shona determined to change her personal future. She wanted to flee immediately, but knew for a clean getaway she had to stay and prepare properly. Her plan was to complete all preparations that night, leave for school as usual in the morning, and never return.

She heard someone begin vacuuming downstairs. That was unheard of so late in the evening. She knew something unusual was happening. Shona hastened downstairs as quickly as she could, and peered through the crack in the hinges of the open door. Rupert was vacuuming, and her mother clearing tables in a rush to make the place presentable for visitors.

Her gut instinct kicked in, she knew they had moved the day forward. Fight or flight? This time she had to flee, and quickly, with time ticking against her. She ran up to her room, changed her clothes, and threw others in her backpack. She packed her keepsakes, knowing she would miss some of the video games and music. Dammit. She took the Smartphone, but turned it off so that there would be no tracking signal. She knew she would never return to the house.

Shona intended to slip out the front door while nobody was looking, but just as she opened it, a Town Car pulled up. She closed the front door and ran for the kitchen. The noise of the vacuum died, and she heard footsteps approaching, regardless of the risk, she bolted for the mudroom, and just made it.

She raided the chest freezer, searching the lower levels seldom visited, taking only pre-cooked food. Shona did not know how long her journey would be, or even where she was going.

Her escape was disturbed by voices from the living room. She crept like a feral cat hunting, and listened at the kitchen door. "She should have finally be mine tonight you know, Sally."

The Creepo's words were cut short by her now ex-mother. "Know she never was yours, Rupert. Her maidenhead is worth fifteen thousand dollars to me, and it will be sold tonight. You had better change before they get here. They will do a hymen check, and you can take her later as spoiled goods. You got that?"

Shona was about to cry. The rejection was much too severe. Yet in that moment, a heavy hand slammed the front door. She wondered why he did not use the bell chime, until she glimpsed him from the shadows. The gangster had the look of a predatory animal, and it was chilling.

Shona knew that sort of person only lived to feast off others' ugliest of imagined sins and nightmares, making them their reality. The goon was pure evil in living form.

As Shona made it to the back door she saw a roll of large trash bags on the side. She ripped a couple off, and wrapped them round her backpack. They would cover most of the bright design.

She heard footsteps going up to her ex-bedroom, and slunk out of the back door, locking the dead bolt from outside, and taking the key with her. There was a spare, but it would slow pursuers down. With the front and side of the house covered, she headed out back. She knew there was a gap in the rear hedge that led out to the scrubland behind, and more snakes. That was the only place she could go without being seen. She ran for freedom.

Shona squeezed through and was about to jump a muddy pool, when she remembered the nearby drainage ditch. She looked back and no one was following her, so she carefully strode into the mud, and ran for the water, leaving obvious, muddy tracks veering west.

Once in the ditch, she bolted east, the water used to disguise her trail, but saw a flashlight in the distance headed her way. Knowing she would be spotted, Shona quickly washed off the worst of the mud from her sneakers, realizing there was not much left. With clean soles, she ran for a neighbor's back yard leaving no footprints. She needed to escape the flashlight.

The light turned in her direction, and she dove for the nearest cover. It was a rangy juniper shrub trimmed to fit into the hedge. There was a small gap between the spread of trunks, and Shona knew she could squeeze through if she removed her backpack. Forcing one smaller tree trunk away, she stepped through without looking back.

Chapter 3 – In the Doghouse

Shona froze, hearing a deep growl close by. This was Satan. He was the dopiest of pit bulls once he knew you: Satan and Shona were good friends.

She dropped down squatting, and quietly called him to her. He was unsure, but recognized her whispered voice. She felt his presence sniffing the air, mere inches away from her exposed throat. She was not scared at all, she knew he would never hurt her. He was just alarmed that she was visiting him so late, and probably smelled her fear of being caught.

Shona leaned forward on her haunches to speak to him, touching noses. "Satan, help me. Some nasty people are after me. You will protect me, won't you? Yeah! Of course you will."

The growl changed to a short whining curiosity. She felt his cold wet nose touch her cheek, dragging up into her hair, before he buried his snout into her neck and they cuddled. He was soon licking Shona's face and powering her over onto her back thinking this was a new and exciting game.

Eventually Shona managed to extract herself from his *doggy lurve*, and reaching into her jacket, pulled out a bar of chocolate toffee she had been saving for a special occasion. She guessed this was it. Satan sat as soon as he saw it, attentive, his night-vision being far better than her own. Shona broke off the first hunk and made a slow point of eating it herself.

She would not normally do this, but he needed to know who was in charge, as her life was at stake within this play—in more ways than one. Satan cocked his head to one side, his ears pricked, and his brow furrowed with anticipation. He pawed the air with entreaty as his jowls drooled.

Shona broke off a second hunk and slowly offered it to him. She had to stifle a giggle as the gooey toffee innards got stuck in his teeth. Satan gnashed the air, trying to eat it properly, his goopy saliva drenching the ground as he shook his head in combined euphoria and desperation.

In her old back yard a few doors down, she heard some henchman-gorilla shout, "Over here, the young bitch went through this gap, help me break it down."

Shona dove for cover in the first available place, Satan's outdoor kennel. She had laughed when she first saw it, shaped like a small windowless house with pitched roof, and an offset hole at one side for a door.

Once inside she could see several lights sweep Satan's yard from outside, but she remained out of direct view. Satan immediately turned to challenge them, this time his growl and bared teeth carried the conviction of deathly menacing intent.

The kennel was quite nice, in a doggy sort of way, although it reeked of concentrated, unwashed canine. Shona was trapped. She needed to get out, and before dawn would be good. But for now she was safe. She caught snatches of conversation from the men, one said, "Her tracks lead to the ditch, she must have escaped using it to cover her trail, but in which direction?

Another yelled with intimidation, "Cover both, you idiot, the young slut has to be around here somewhere. Milo, take teams to check all the nearby houses. Start with the back yards. I'll call Lynch, tell him to bring his lads over to help out."

Shona needed a diversion, so without considering implications, called 911. "I just avoided being raped by my mother's boyfriend. I am thirteen years old. My mother's address is..."

The inquisition began. They wanted to keep her talking, and what they were asking was anything but comforting. The light dawned; they were tracing her cell. Her father had been right. She cut the call and turned the Smartphone off immediately, and hoped she had acted before they managed to triangulate her precise location. Shona removed the battery. "Trace that then." It seemed to her that cops and bad guys were all in the same business. They just did things in a different way.

A few minutes later, she heard cars arrive, followed by sirens in the distance, and there were a lot of them. She knew she had just made a big mistake. Both the hoods and the police would now be looking for her. She felt so stupid.

Out on the street, tires screeched to a halt as a Town Car burned rubber to escape. Automatic fire followed and shots rang out in response. Shona could see the resultant fireball as a gas tank blew. It turned out to be one of the patrol cars, the officer cursing the remains of his vehicle, "I'll kill you for wrecking my cruiser, you son of a bitch."

The next voice she heard was familiar, and for once terrified, "Let go of me you thug, we are not going with you. This is our home."

Her ex-mother's voice was cut off as a series of car doors slammed shut. The hoods fled the scene, firing what must have been a missile launcher to take out another cop cruiser. They seemed to make good their escape, as there was a moment of total silence, before the cops swarmed everywhere.

Just like the hoods, they also started going house to house searching for her. Cops even tried to look in her kennel, but Satan denied them, twice, both times rising ferociously to protect her, and ignoring his owner's commands to stand down. Satan came inside with her, and growled from his doorway at anyone who approached. The cops went away, saying they would be back tomorrow. They left the yard but not the neighborhood.

She thought that God, if he, or she, or it existed, must have been looking out for her that night.

She saw the SWAT team arrive to take the house, her former home, and found it empty. Shona's eyes were drooping as Satan, in his element, stood guard outside. He was reveling in the action, and proud to be a Dog. Shona had never felt so safe and secure in all her life, except for when her father last held her—and that had been far too long ago. That comforting memory sent her to sleep. Later she became aware of a large, black, furry bulk nestling to sleep with her.

Shona was semi-woken several times, when Satan launched to protect her. He growled and barked with venom at all who ventured near his territory.

Come daylight, John Welbourne, his owner, called Satan for their morning walk, but the dog remained unmoved. He had his secret to protect. From deep within the safety of the kennel, Shona could see John give the dog an odd look, before setting down his breakfast bowl and standing to watch. Later he fussed his truest and only companion.

Cruisers returned a short while later and another search was underway. Shona curled into a sitting ball, a small blue thing, her back against the inside hard wood at the front of the kennel. The opening was on the other side, offering her complete seclusion, unless somebody actually poked their head inside. They tried, but every time Satan denied them.

The voices receded at last, but Shona waited, and waited, and waited. Later, John appeared once more and called Satan to him.

Chapter 3

Shona snuck a peek and he was alone. The autos pulled away, except for the constant presence next door at her former home.

John looked at the dog kennel, and absentmindedly said to Satan, "Now what do you know, that nobody else does?" He patted the dog on the head and added, "Clever Dog."

He was quiet for some time as he stroked the head of his trustworthy friend. Shona saw him look over towards her last home, next to the street, the rear hedge, and back to the dog's kennel. He nodded his head and returned inside, leaving the door open for Satan to follow, but he did not.

Shona was bored, cramped, and needed to stretch, but she reasoned she must stay where she was until darkness fell. Her heart was heavy and her emotions almost got the better of her. Sometimes she cried unbidden; she missed her mother, her home, her things. She would be leaving her friends behind, and felt scared of the unknown that awaited footsteps away.

Mostly, she was traumatized her mother had been about to sell her as an underage sex slave. Her tears dried immediately, and were replaced by anger, revulsion. Her heart hardened, she had made the right decision. She had to be brave and see it through.

She thought of her father, and how he described the life of the outlaw. Visions of old western movies, gunfighters flitted through her mind, but that was not what he meant. He had told her to stand up for herself, without regard, and do what she felt was right for her; except for hurting the innocent.

Remembering his last words, she felt comforted and spoke aloud, if whispering, "I'm gonna take a ride on my luck, put my feet on the road, and no looking back—'cept for you, Dad."

Shona pointed and said "You." Satan rose and licked her outstretched forefinger and thumb, before enveloping her hand in his gloopy mouth; 'was this a new game?'. Extracting her hand and shaking off the excess saliva, she realized time had already moved on.

Eventually, she began to think about her predicament, since she had only escaped all of fifty-yards so far. Nonetheless, she remained free. If she made a run for it before nightfall, she was sure to be spotted.

She drifted in and out of stress-filled sleep for most of the morning. She loved the times Satan nuzzled, and snuggled next to her. She wrapped her arms and legs around her protector. Later, she was starving and in her bag, the food had thawed. She shared with Satan, but discovered she had nothing to drink. Fool! She was learning about survival, and quickly.

A little later, a curious thing occurred. John came out and walked around the backyard. Satan's water bowl was set well over to the side of the house, in the shade near the patio door. John picked it up as Shona watched through bleary eyes, and started to nod off again. Shona zoned out, her existence was *mega boring*.

A moment afterward, a sound brought her fully awake, that of someone scuffing the turf nearby. "Here's your clean water, Satan." John placed it right next to the entrance to the kennel, just to one side. The dog went to drink the cool liquid, but John called him away immediately to play a game.

Shona had the idea John knew she was there, but he was playing a game with her, as well as Satan. She watched and they walked away from her. Shona reached out, desperate to drink. She could smell the washing-up liquid on the inside of the dog bowl. She was so thirsty it would not have mattered if it had reeked of Satan's slobber, if one time only.

She came alert around midday, but when she peeked outside she still saw far too many people, and the media had arrived in force. That all changed some hours later, when they had gotten all they could get, and departed. John wandered out and stood nearby, squatting down to retrieve Satan's water bowl. He said in normal voice, "My Satan, you sure are thirsty today."

Shona thought him done, but he whispered, "I know you are in there Shona. Satan is a clever dog. The cops are coming back with search warrants, so we do not have much time to get you out of there, and to a real place of safety.

"I would never do this for your mother, the bitch, but your father came to see me a few days ago. We go back a long ways. Bill asked me to keep an eye out for you, so trust me please, and do what I say. We did our Marine training together, and he saved my life once, Nicaragua, which you may not know. I owe him, and will see no harm comes to you. All I need you to do is trust me. Capisce?"

He did not wait for Shona to reply, but left her to figure it out for herself.

Shona remembered her father saying he was going to meet his old buddy John, before he took his freedom trip. She knew this

Chapter 3

man was the same John, who would have the burner cell her father left for her. John had told her father the nearby house was for sale, and when Mother (ex-mother) wanted to buy it, she agreed. Shona never told her mother that their new neighbor was her father's good friend; that was a secret between the three of them.

Shona realized she should have gone to him first, but secrecy died hard, and she had thought she could handle her mother and Creepo herself. She never knew her father had saved the man's life. Her decision was made.

Shona was expecting release to come within minutes, but it did not. Instead, John cut the hedge. She had no idea what his plan was, until he backed his pickup onto the rear lawn, nearly up to Satan's kennel, and started filling it with the clippings. He came around back and stated quietly, "Shona, it is time to move. I need you to dive under the pickup, and hold on to a crossbeam near the front. I will drag you out, and get you inside by the side door when the coast is clear. Wait for me to open the door, and call you, OK?"

She started to reply, but he was already gone. Shona put her backpack into one of the trash liners she had used to disguise it, and dove for new cover. She could see John's feet, so threw the backpack nearby. He picked it up and walked away. She found the crossbeam, and got good handholds.

The drag, when it came, was a bit like a ride in an amusement park, and Shona wanted to do it again. This was so exciting. Evasion in broad daylight. She loved their game, but knew it would end all too soon. Anyway, she had to get properly away.

Shona waited for the side door to open, but instead a cop poked his nose in, asking, "You seen a young girl around here, Shona Waverly, lives a few doors down ... What are you taking away? ... You don't mind if I take a look, here's the search warrant..."

Obviously, they had eyes everywhere, and on everybody. Why had she been so stupid as to call them?

The cops had search warrants for everything in the neighborhood, and first checked out John's rear yard, and this time Satan allowed them to inspect his home. That is not to say he was at all happy about it. He barked up a storm but this time he obeyed his master's voice.

Finding zip, they returned to the pickup, and emptied everything out of the back of John's truck bed, looking for her.

John had pulled up real close to the back door, so they could only throw the clippings out the side or back, which built a barrier between Shona and them. She began to think John was quite clever, already knowing what the cops would most-likely do.

The Sergeant appeared, and tried to look under John's truck. Shona found footholds and raised herself off the ground as high as she could. The cop's back creaked as he bent over, and with all the clippings in the way, only took a cursory glance. They had done it. The cops moved on to the next house.

A few minutes later Shona heard the side, screen door unlock, and John came out. He squeezed through the small gap between the pickup and the wall, and once he had a clear view of the street said, "Go now Shona."

She made it inside, and he followed close behind. She thought their game was over, but there was another play.

John gave her the burner cell her father had left as soon as they got inside. He also gifted her a hiker's backpack, a brand new one that had a solar panel for charging cell phones by day. He gave her his old Army canteen, but said he wanted it back, sometime. Water was the most essential thing for life, something she had recently discovered.

Later that evening they hit the road. Shona was hunkered down under the dashboard. They drove slowly up the road, and both knew the detectives in the nearby cruiser were watching them. John wanted to get the cops off their tail before the thought to follow the pickup even dawned within their scalloptic skulls.

After checking the rearview, John said, "We're being followed. They must not have enough to do tonight. Reach round for the rug on the back seat, and keep your head down. Cover yourself with it, and everything will be fine. I need them to check us out on my terms, not theirs."

They pulled into a nearby gas station, John telling Satan, "On guard." He blipped the locks, and topped off with gas. He left the pickup unattended, and sauntered inside to pay, and buy snacks for a journey, like everybody does. They alone already knew the tank was nearly full, so he only put in ten dollars worth, implying to any observers that he was not intending on going a long way.

Shona watched as best she could, and saw one Suit follow him inside, as outside the other walked over to inspect their pickup truck.

Chapter 3

The plain clothes cop shone his flashlight inside the cab. He came face to face with Satan, who was not at all impressed with his enquiry. Shona's protector bared his teeth, and made a low and menacing, guttural growl. The cop pulled away, but continued to inspect the truck, from a greater distance.

She heard John say, "Young man, do you know the way to Valinda? Sir, I can tell you are a Child of Jesus. Let me tell you of His Word, for therein lies our only path to righteousness and salvation…"

The monologue continued as John became the essence of a Sunday Morning, God-slot preacher.

John was chuckling to himself when he came back to open the driver's door, and fired the engine.

Shona asked him, "What happened in there?"

John explained, "Shona, we needed out of this situation fast, but I knew that saying, 'Keep the change' would save two-seconds only, and raise suspicion from the cop that followed me into the store.

"As a diversion, I asked the cashier, 'Heah. Do you know the quickest way to Valinda? Come dawn, I have a job to do there for our church, and it's new to me.'

"The attendant was blunt and negatory, as I expected. Shona, I turned and asked the same of the Suit, who ignored me and moved away, as if he was not interested. I pretended to wander casually outside, all my instincts alive, and headed back for the pickup. My interest was only focused on the second cop; I hid it well, you heard the rest."

Shona noticed the cops had hurried off, wanting nothing more to do with them. His alibi was secure and they were moving again, before doubling back around.

Shona liked the way John talked, thought; a sort of mixture of professor and the hard-boiled detective stories her father used to read. She watched his face, and it was a picture of victorious subterfuge. His eyes were alive with intent. Their game was on, large.

The minutes dragged until John let Shona choose the radio station. They spoke of her immediate plans, and he offered her many alternatives and good advice. But just like her father, Shona knew the only safe place was off the grid. John tried to persuade her to consider better options, but her mind was set. Shona would follow in her father's footsteps, come what may.

John talked her out of heading for Vegas, and insisted she head south, even though they were traveling north. He said, "Your Father taught me this, so never forget, Shona. Always head in the wrong direction until you know it is safe. When you are sure, head indirectly for your intended destination. Double back if you think you are being followed. Leave a clue when you can to throw off any followers, like switch on your cell, or use an ATM, so the authorities think they are tracking you. Take your money, whatever, switch off, and move sideways until the coast is clear. Do you understand what I am telling you? This was all part and parcel of how Bill, your father, saved my life."

He clammed up, not wanting to speak further. Shona knew that memories of a war he would rather forget haunted him.

After eons, they abruptly came to a halt in a shower of gravel. Shona imagined the sound was shrapnel bouncing off the underside of the pickup. They had arrived.

Her mind became detached somehow, and she realized all she saw was darkness, and the intrusive bright lights of the unknown and indefinable. They echoed the way she felt, blind, small, and vulnerable.

The truck stop was dirty and dingy, and would be most unappealing to her ex-mother. Shona liked it at once. Her body was sore and aching. She felt banged up, and thought he would find a rig.

John told her to wait. She did not know where she was, but it was a long way aways from where she did not want to be. She was dead center of Nowhere.

He came back a minute later with two doggy bags, he gave one to Satan, and the other to her. It was the best burger treat the truck stop had on offer, and she wolfed it down—Satan competing to see who would finish first. Shona knew Satan thought he won, but he didn't drink the cola.

Shona was distracted when John said with finality, "Keep off the grid. Use the railcars at the siding behind here, and always go in the wrong direction until you know you are safe. Here."

He gave her a roll of twenty dollar bills, and said, "Pay me back, if and when you can. I am doing this for you, and your father. It's time for you to go, make good your escape."

Chapter 3

It all seemed a bit sudden. She stared at the blackness, and would in moments be a part of it. John came around as Shona closed the passenger door from the outside, and he settled the backpack on her shoulders. The electronic lock bleeped.

Footsteps walked away; they were paired two and four.

Far away, a lonesome whistle blew. It was time for Shona to step into the unknown, to discover her own future for herself.

Chapter 4 – Rosa's Store

The freight trains were dire, and the inhabitants tricksters, fakesters, and lecherous numbskulls of all ages and persuasions. Shona kept to herself 'catching-out', as the hobos called hopping trains. She endured, and survived. One or two tried to befriend her, others tried to maul her. She kept well clear of them all.

Some migrants got off to get jobs picking fruit in the rolling hills to the east of San Diego. She had no destination in mind, but understood most of their Spanish. She needed a change of scenery, so took a chance by following their Cuadrilla. Unlike most of the other losers, these men and women were trying to make a living, undocumented but honestly.

She didn't join their small group, but followed them. The dusty animal track wound interminably uphill, for miles, until they arrived at a derelict building at the edge of a small, dilapidated town. They set up camp and she watched them for a while, until they seemed to settle for the night. She got her hoodie out and wore it, even though the night was stiflingly hot and humid. She zipped it up tight, and pulled the cover over so only the smallest part of her face showed.

The nearby—and only—store was a rundown sprawl that, from the outside, looked like it needed a good cleaning. The sign above the door was flaking paint, but Shona made out the name, "Rosa's," and went inside. She grabbed a bottle of water from the cooler, and with a wave to the woman behind the till, opened it and drank deeply. She was parched after the long hike.

Feeling more human, she reviewed her situation one last time, and knew she needed to change her appearance. She needed to look eighteen and full of attitude, so decided to become a goth. She loved her long blonde hair, but it had to go.

There were boxes and half-stocked shelves everywhere, as if someone had started to restock them, before being interrupted. She grabbed cheap and filling ready-food, and was on the lookout for cockroaches and rats, but the store was actually quite clean beneath the chaos.

Shona picked up scissors, a couple of cheap plastic mirrors, and some blacker-than-black hair dye. She grabbed some of the most awful makeup, all black, purple, maroon, and blue. She saw an orange eyebrow pencil and knew it was for her. She needed razor blades to remove her eyebrows, and added some ghostly-white face powder to complete the look. Changing herself was getting quite complicated but she wanted to do it right.

There was a strange Catholic shrine near the checkout, and adjacent, some weird pendants with runes of pagan significance. She grabbed a couple of the most outrageous and set her basket down, hoping to get out of the hellhole as quickly as possible. The woman behind the counter took her time ringing up the purchases. She could feel the woman's eyes upon her, but kept her face covered and looked either down or away from the cashier, pretending, eventually, to look at the store.

Shona need not have bothered. The woman spoke to her in Spanish, which Shona tried to ignore, but in time replied to. She was not all that good at the language, so kept her words simple and correctly enunciated. The woman laughed and told her the price, which was extortionate. Shona rose belligerently to confront her, her wad already in her fist.

Horror-struck, the woman covered her hand and scolded, "Put that money away immediately, child. If anyone sees it, know it will be gone before you know it."

The cashier stood back for a moment as Shona hid the money John had given her, and the woman nodded her head. All of a sudden, Shona realized the woman had spoken to her in English. She needed to get a lot better at this, and fast. The cashier took her basket and set it aside, canceling the transaction with a flick of her finger.

The woman's eyes were slightly rheumy as she turned away and crossed herself at the strange Catholic shrine. She took a new basket and walked the aisles, filling it with many items. There was something strange about the way she treated Shona. The woman was not ingratiating, more bossy, but in a motherly sort of way. Casually she looked back at Shona as if measuring her.

The woman dropped two of the most awful bra and panty sets into the new carrier, and said, "These are too big for you, for what are you, fourteen? It doesn't matter. Here is a thread and needle pack. Use it and the scissors to make them fit, but allow for growth. I suggest you don't cut, but sew. You can sew, can't you? Each has secret waterproof pockets, three in all per set. Keep your important stuff inside and forget about how they look. Keep your money out of sight child. D'you hear me?"

Shona nodded her head, and the woman continued, "My advice is to keep only a few dollars in your ordinary pockets, and spread them around. Now, I have seen you on the news. You are from Compton, LA, right." It was not a question, but a statement.

The woman teased a wisp of Shona's hair and felt it before saying, "The hair dye you chose is no good for your hair. You don't need the mirrors either, for why would you want to look at yourself?" Shona could have taken offense, except she needed to know what the woman was up to.

The cashier got a different dye from the shelves. Shona was warming to her, if only because she kept on talking about nothing. The glint in the woman's eye returned when they got back to the counter, before she rang up the new total.

However, before telling her the charge, she said, "My last employee left three weeks ago, which is why the place is a total mess. He used to catch the rats out back and we sold them to the itinerants as food. Now, the rats are thriving in the garbage."

The owner weighed her words carefully before continuing. "I was about your age when I went on the run, and I ended up here." She crossed herself and looked at Shona deeply, before adding, "Sometimes we all need to grasp the future, take our chances, and never look back."

Shona was stunned. The last time she saw her father, he said virtually those same words to her. A shadow crossed Shona's heart, one she knew could easily reopen recent wounds. She tried to blot the thoughts, the images away, and scrunched up her face with evasion. The woman read Shona well, and spoke, "My name is Rosa, and I own this place."

She waited for Shona's full attention. "I need help for about one month, thirty-three days if all goes well. I can pay you nothing in return. However, I can give you food and provide shelter, a safe place for you to live, far away from prying eyes, which is what you want, is it not?"

Shona nodded her head, gradually realizing that she was not only being offered a job, but security. "You will work sixteen hours each day, like I do, every day, but it is not hard work. I will change your appearance, provide you with food and a bed, and, if you shape up, teach you some survival skills. Run away now and I won't say a thing. Run away after we agree and I will turn you in.

Chapter 4

"So here's the deal. You will work for me, for free, for thirty-three days, learn what you can about survival in that time, and at the end of it I will owe you nothing."

Shona was about to get upset, until she looked into the owner's eyes, and something within Rosa moved Shona. For no great reason, Shona shrugged her shoulders and said, "OK."

Spanish exploded from Rosa's lips, as if a new dawn had risen. She locked the store door for the moment, and led Shona through to the rear. The main storeroom was a greater mess than the store, but the living area was clean and tidy. Shona's new bedroom reminded her of a prison cell, a simple bed, drawers, nightstand, and one high, rusted window with broken glass panes.

She slept for a while, all her clothes left on. The knock on her door came just after eleven, when Rosa closed the store. Shona followed her into the main room, and Rosa asked, "Tell me how you want your new look to be."

Shona didn't have much of a clue, truth be known, but answered, "Cut my hair, but with attitude, like straight and keep my ears covered. No bangs, points at the side of my face, hair black."

They continued to talk as Rosa cut her hair, but not as drastically as Shona would have done herself. The hair dye was applied and Rosa said, "This dye will take an hour or more to work on your hair. Come, help me cook supper, and you may learn something new."

Shona followed Rosa into the kitchen where she cooked, and Shona prepped following her instructions. It was fun because Rosa was also teaching her how to cook Mexican food. They dished-up, and while it tasted strange, it was tasty. She ate everything and was allowed to go back to the kitchen for seconds. She already felt good about her choice of new home, and hoped it would last.

Shona was stuffed by the time they finished the dessert, and all she wanted to do was curl up on her bed. Instead Rosa said, "It has been ninety minutes already girl, and we both need to sleep. Hurry up so we can rinse out the color."

At last, they washed out the dye, and Shona was shocked. She looked completely different. Rosa stared at her for a while before saying, "Your idea of goth will suit you. Here, let me show you how it is done."

By the time Rosa had finished, Shona swore she was staring into the face of an eighteen-year old stranger. Rosa spoke, "Chiquita, that means little girl, and other things you will learn about. Look in the mirror, for this is a simple template for you to develop into your new self. I hope you like it."

All of a sudden, Shona did not feel like a little girl anymore. She felt like an adult meeting the world, at last, on her own terms. "Awesome, this is so wicked, I love it."

Shona hugged Rosa in thanks. Apart from her father and John, no one had ever been so kind to her. People say, 'you can't choose your family, but you can choose your friends'. Untrue. Shona had chosen her own family members, and her birth mother was no longer any part of it.

Later, alone in her room, Shona mused, "I wonder who my new mother will be. Do I even need one anymore? Now, that is why the proteen world of a girl is pretty screwed, right?"

Rosa woke her a few hours later as dawn blanched the night sky. Shona felt so tired she could have slept for sixteen hours a day and only been awake for eight, but it was not to happen. In the days that followed, she cleaned the store, stocked shelves, and got rid of the mess. Rosa taught her Mexican cooking, and how to catch rats to sell to the migrant workers as protein to supplement their meager diet. It was tough at first, until Shona got her head around it. They spoke a weird sort of Mexican Spanish with local overtones. The worst of it was, they only ever spoke Spanish.

Once Shona had sorted the store, storeroom, and garbage, Rosa let her handle the cash register. Shona knew Rosa was watching her, and never thought to cheat her. Why would she? By the end of the first week, Rosa trusted her enough to run the store while she had a siesta, and Shona got a few hours off after. Rosa ran the place like a family-owned store, and Shona became her latest daughter.

They closed early on Sunday, so Rosa could go to church. Shona went to bed to catch up on her sleep. The next morning, when Rosa woke her, she said something weird, "Chiquita, last night a close friend of mine told me there is a bona fide name for sale: April Bekkons. She is dead, but there are ways around the system. Do you want that name?"

Rosa could see Shona was still groggy, so left her to think it over, while she went off to cook breakfast and prep for lunch.

Chapter 4

'April Bekkons', it sounded like 'spring beckons', and Shona liked it at once. Like new and verdant growth, a new start for her in a brand new world. From that day onwards, most people only knew of her as April.

Shona stayed for almost two months in all. She learned a lot, the local Spanish in particular. How to spot a thief in the store, how to catch rats like an expert, and much more. Eventually, Rosa's niece and nephew, Marisol and Pepe, managed to cross the border. Rosa disappeared for almost two whole days when she went to fetch them.

Shona ran the store like a pro in Rosa's absence, always on the lookout for freeloaders. She caught several and imitated Rosa as they tried to sneak out the door, blocking it physically and making them hand her the goods, banning them for several days as the whim took her. It was fun. She knew some things went missing, but about the same as usual.

Marisol and Pepe arrived late at night as she was preparing to close the store. Rosa wanted to close at once, but Shona said she would handle it. There was an old guy with them, a local man called Uncle Tepin.

Shona had seen him several times before, and apparently, he had done the driving. He and Rosa seemed to be more than good friends, and she wondered if Tepin was one of Rosa's old boyfriends. She did not know if anything had ever happened between them, but neither could she be sure that something had not.

They had a great party that night, a family reunion. Shona joined them for a short while, but she was exhausted. She woke at six as usual, and realized they were still celebrating. She cooked Mexican for them, and laid a table full of what she thought they might like to eat.

Chapter 5 – April Bekkons

Shona stayed on for a couple more weeks, training Marisol and Pepe in what to do. In truth, she liked being there, it was safe, and she had nowhere else to go.

Shona was by then thinking, and sometimes dreaming in their version of Spanish. Marisol discovered Shona's birthday was in late July, and they threw a surprise party for her, celebrating late into the night, Pepe and Marisol making it great fun.

Some days later, she watched the store as Marisol and Pepe ate their evening meal. Tepin arrived to join them, he was carrying a folder, and went through to the kitchen where Rosa was cooking. Some time later the cousins relieved Shona, and she joined Rosa and Tepin for dinner. The old man mentioned the upcoming harvest, and Rosa said, "We are already into August, have you thought about what you are going to do with your life, April?"

Shona had not thought about it, she was happy and secure. She looked up, unsure of what to say, and saw the twinkle in Rosa's eyes, the same baiting smile she had used when she asked Shona to work for her. Shona knew Rosa was up to something and replied, "No, I love being here. You're like a mother to me."

Rosa responded straight away. "Good, thank you. Then as your nominated Mother, I think it is time you continued your education. You are clever, hard working, have an excellent memory, and will pass for eighteen with no difficulty."

Rosa watched as Shona's brow creased, as she tried to think it through. She was about to reply when Rosa said, "There are still vacancies at SDSU [San Diego State University]. You already told me you wanted to go to college one day, and that day has arrived."

Shona could not believe Rosa had just said that, her thoughts scattered. How? Why? When? It was impossible, wasn't it?

Rosa read her extremely well, and again spoke just before Shona could muster the words, "April, Tepin has told me ROTC have a few scholarships going begging, and that will pay for your tuition, accommodation, and give you a little spending money— they call it a text book allowance. All we need to do is confirm your new identity, and that costs. You want me to fix it for you?"

Shona gulped the air, her mind racing within opportunities and impossibility. She spluttered her confusion aloud, "But Rosa, I already have a new identity."

Chapter 5

Rosa corrected at once, "No, you do not. You are currently using the name of a dead girl." Rosa stopped to cross herself and bow her head, before she continued speaking. "She came from a remote part of New Mexico."

Shona crossed her arms and sat back, not looking at them. "Becoming a dead person isn't something I ever planned on doing, not just yet, anyways."

She worked out the probabilities, and looked up at Rosa, who now had a slightly concerned look on her face. Shona asked, "Who was she? Tell me. How did she die?"

Rosa tried to dismiss the question, but Shona did not intend to officially take the name of somebody she knew nothing about. Finally, Rosa said, "She was eighteen when she passed on, almost nineteen. She was talking on her cell, while waiting at a bus stop. The front nearside tire of a truck blew, and it ploughed into where she was waiting, demolishing the shelter. I was told she died instantly."

Shona shook her head. This was more than personal, to her at least. She could accept the girl did not suffer, and that settled her somewhat. On the other hand, she still knew zilch about April Bekkons. Shona pestered Rosa until she gave out, "This is all I know, and I advise you never to go asking questions.

"The truck wasn't an ordinary one, it was a U.S. Marshal's or Sheriff's office prisoner transport, I forget which. The authorities wanted the whole thing brushed under the carpet as quickly as possible, and with help from higher powers, they succeeded. However, in their haste to distance any authority from culpability for the death, they missed a few things."

Shona was feeling a bit better, but needed more information, before taking a dead girl's life as her own ... it was kind of personal, for both of them.

Finally Rosa gave in to Shona's repeated inquiries, and explained, "April's father was an electrician and ran his own company. Her mother owned a successful internet café, and they both worked mainly in Santa Fe, although they lived detached on a ranch near Espanola. That is all I know.

"April, wake up! This is a great chance for you. Take it or leave it, what will you do, eh? Become a somebody, or a nobody?"

Shona blanched, she had already asked herself the same question.

"The girl had full identity, including a driver's license for cars, and another for motorbikes. Her academic record was pretty good, and good enough to get you into college. Do you want me to make this a real identity for you?"

Shona sat there stunned. She looked at Rosa, and then at Tepin, who was grinning back at her, a cheroot extruding from his few remaining, blackened teeth. She knew they had fixed this up between them. She also knew they had her. How could she say "No?" Shona could warp four years into the future. Yeah!

She didn't think about it anymore. She pumped the air and shouted, "Yesss!"

Rosa cautioned, "This is expensive, maybe ten thousand dollars or more, but it will all be as good as legal. You will owe me this money, and we will work out later how you will pay me back. Agreed? Your word of honor, or hope to die?"

Shona made the vow before them, and felt great inside. Tepin spoke to her for the first time, "April, I need you to sign this form."

She was giddy with excitement, and signed her name the way she always did. The old man laughed and said, "Just as well I brought along a spare form, April Bekkons."

Shona stared at the sheet she had signed, and saw the name "Shona Waverly" staring back at her. How dumb was she? Time to wise-up!

Tepin showed her a copy of the dead girl's ID, and she liked the way the girl had written her name immediately. Shona embellished it through practice, to make it her own name, and signed the forms Tepin asked her to.

Rosa said, "There is just one more thing to make this a real ID, we will need to register you as a Californian citizen. I will ask the local Sheriff to call round sometime tomorrow and take your fingerprints for the record, and that is all there is to it."

Tepin interjected, "They only need your thumbprint officially, but a full set provided by the cops always stops anyone asking awkward questions. Trust me, I have done this several times before. By rights, they may want to see you in person, but I think we can get around that. I will need some photographs though, April, without your goth make-up on, please."

He tapped the side of his head knowingly, and grinned. Although Shona was worried about having her fingerprints taken, she hugged both of them in a flurry of heartfelt gratitude. That night excitement and doubts haunted her, keeping her awake for half the night, or so it seemed.

The next morning she had other worries, as Tepin dropped by with some old question sheets. Shona had to study how to pass the ROTC induction examination, and entry procedures for SDSU. Without help, she was lost. She could not turn on her Smartphone, or she would give her location away. She needed a new number to surf the internet, and that would cost a bomb.

There was not much choice. She spoke to Rosa and explained her predicament. Rosa said, "Give me your cell and I will get you a 'pay-as-you-go' sim card to match. The guy will need to unblock the network lock, so it can be used by any sim card." Shona nodded her head in understanding, since this was the root of her problem.

Shona went back to thoughts about her father, wondering how he was, and what he was doing. She sent him a wish, hoping he was OK. While her mind was absorbed, Rosa called Tepin. It turned out he was busy for a few hours, but would drop by again later. Shona's proteen nature resurfaced, "This is so unfair…"

Her outburst was cut short when a Hispanic voice asked, "And what is 'so unfair' young lady? April Bekkons, I presume?"

Rosa stood to shake the Deputy Sheriff's hand and said, "Manny, my cousin April is hoping to enroll at college, but needs a scholarship or we can't afford it. She is worried about the ROTC assessment exam, and needs to research the likely questions online at an internet café or library."

The cop looked at Shona approvingly and said, "Undersheriff Teves at your service, Ma'am. My pleasure to meet you officially, although I have seen you working this store for several months. We talked on a couple of occasions, remember?"

Shona replied in kind, and Teves took her prints before taking a coffee from the machine and relaxing. He spoke to Rosa about local matters, before coming back to Shona, asking her where she was from. Remembering the dead girl's documents, Shona replied, "Santa Fe, up near Espanola, if you know it?"

Teves shook his head disarmingly, before adding, "Never heard of Espanola, but I know Santa Fe. They got a nice new airport up there nowadays, or so I hear."

Rosa was standing almost behind him, and Shona saw her alarm, shaking her head vigorously in denial. Shona replied, "No, they had plans for one, but they got shelved, like everything else in Santa Fe. That's why I need an education, to get the hell out of there and make something of my life. To do that, I need to pass the ROTC exam, so I can get a scholarship."

Shona hunched her shoulders as if it was all too much for her, and looked down. Teves spoke into the silence, "I admire you. You want to do something with your life, not like most of the deadbeats that cross my path. I tell you what, I'll give you a lift to the library in Jamal."

Shona did not want to go with him, but Teves was persuasive. She knew he wanted to get her alone, to check her out. During the ride, she answered his initial thrusts with good memory, before asking him about his own career, and how he chose to become a cop. It turned out he had also been through ROTC. It had been his key to getting accepted as a recruit into the Sheriff's Office.

They pulled up outside the library, and Shona made to get out at once. Teves turned to her and said, "April, I like you, and I respect your ambition. I still have some friends in ROTC, and, no promises, but I will mention your name to them, OK?

"Oh, and April, lose the goth war-paint, they prefer their own." His conspiratorial smile beamed, enlivened by his traditional looking Mexican moustache, and with kind words of parting, she escaped at last.

Relief flooded through her, she had survived the interrogation. Shona felt good about herself, as she watched the cruiser depart.

From that moment, time flashed by in a flourish of wistful intensity. The days passed, and through it all, Rosa stood firm and kept Shona on track. She did begin to think of Rosa as her new mother, if only because she acted like one. Her father always let her get away with all sorts of stuff. Rosa did not.

On the day Shona was due to leave, Rosa did her roots and made her up like a true goth-chick. It took several hours, while she reminded Shona how to apply the makeup, first the gray, followed by wraithlike shades, finally the white face streaks. The dapples, being one of the hardest to get right. It had to have that *Ghostly* quality, as hints and splashes of deeper and deepest gray showed through. It was awesome.

God, did Shona look so old! And more importantly, she looked nothing like the person the hoods and cops were looking for. She was free.

Chapter 5

Rosa disappeared for an hour with Tepin, but returned and accompanied her to the bus stop. Shona thought she would only stay a moment to say goodbye. Instead, Rosa slipped an envelope into her hand and said, "Use this to enroll at SDSU. It will keep you off the grid, confirm your new identity, and keep you safe. Dearest child, come back and see me sometimes."

Rosa gripped her arm tightly, wilted, and drew Shona into her bosom like a real mother would. Moments later, Rosa broke the embrace and wiped her tears, as if she had just lost a treasure. Her emotions getting the better of her, Rosa turned her back, and never once looked over her shoulder. Partings between true friends, family, should always be like this.

Only ever look back if you are unsure and can't hide the fact, or fancy the guy to pieces. Shona reckoned that was fourteen going on Socrates.

Shona was dying to look in the envelope, but waited until she was completely alone and out of sight of *el stupido* Bus-Cam. The contents were astonishing. She had a full U.S. passport in the name of April Bekkons, a driver's license for bikes, and another for cars. Each was legitimate. She cried. "Big Girl Me. Yeah! Right."

Shona stared at the documents with wonder and trepidation. She was about to commit to a life plan, and there was no going back. What would her father think? She answered this with another question, "What would my ex-mother, or slimy-snake Sicko do, if they ever discovered me?"

Her mind made up on the spur of the moment, Shona wholeheartedly embraced her new name, 'April'. It felt like a right of passage, a spring into the future that locked her past life forever behind her, and opened a new door to her adult future.

Shona Waverly had gotten on the bus in front of Rosa's store. April Bekkons stepped off the bus near the main SDSU campus, and stopped-dead. The air felt fresh. It was alive with the sense of expectation, something new, and something unknowable—unless she gathered her abruptly waning courage, to walk bravely and purposefully forwards.

This was it, to boldly embrace her potential, her future as April Bekkons, or become another "have not." Seeing losers all around, she placed one foot in front of the other, and never looked back.

Chapter 6 – A New Life

April met bureaucracy immediately, because she had to enroll with ROTC and SDSU at the same time. Fourteen year old Shona would have thought it was quite stupid; nineteen year old April realized it was the price of admission to her future. Both induction facilities had admin offices on campus, but they were seemingly miles apart. She stopped for a drink, and noticed a heathen girl get a soda from the machine.

They both looked at their cells, and rose to leave at the same time. They were headed in the same direction, at the same time, separately. It was such an odd feeling; April knew instinctively, they were going to the same place, probably for the same reason.

April made a point of entering the ROTC building first, but waited to hold the door open for the other girl. She let go as soon as the heathen's foot came level with the far side of the door, the girl said, "Thanks, bitch."

April paid her no mind. Opening a door for yourself is one thing; waiting on another to pass through and go before you is completely different. April was going to be first, and the other girl could follow in her wake, or not, as suited the heathen's ego best. It mattered not to April.

They ended up in the same lines, filled out the same forms, and were processed the same. April's initial interview went well, until the recruitment sergeant asked her, "So tell me April, why do you want to join the Army?"

Her reasons were patently obvious. She could have said, "I need a new identity and acceptance. I need a scholarship to pay for my future education, and I need to do something with my life."

April had never considered joining the Army as a career move, but it was a means to an end. She did not speak her thoughts aloud, instead she said, "I had it rough as a kid. I respect discipline, and I know how to defend myself. I want to take this many steps further, to gain a good education, and prove myself as an all-American kid; how to protect and serve, how to stand up for our great nation."

She was going to say more, but she had already cracked the code. The sergeant looked up and said, "You came almost top of the assessment, and I would stamp your scholarship right now, but first I need photos. Lose the goth. You hear me? And come back real soon, because I only have a few places left to give away."

Chapter 6

April was out of there like a shot, bully or not, goth or not, sometimes you have to toe the official line, if only to make the imbeciles happy. The heathen girl was waiting outside, next in line. She said, "How'd it go?"

"I gotta lose the goth, and if I'm back in time, I'm in."

For no reason she whispered in the heathen's ear, "There aren't many places left, break a leg."

April didn't know why, but in some strange ways, the girl reminded her of her father. That was a weird thought.

As if putting the face-paint on wasn't bad enough, getting it off in a hurry was a nightmare. When she got back to the interview room, a light was flashing, and the heathen was stood outside the door, blocking it. April was going to ask her how it went, when the girl spoke, "There's just one scholarship left. You owe me 'Hon'."

April was racing against time for the last available money, and knew she owed the girl for blocking the door. If only she had listened to Tepin, to Teves—but then, April was her own girl.

The sergeant processed her quickly, "Tell Teves he owes me. You came highly recommended. Welcome to the Army, Cadet Bekkons."

He rose to salute her. April replied likewise. He smiled as he sat back down behind his desk, and said, "Get your official Army photos done before you do anything else with your face."

She got the photos done, and wondered why she had spent so much time covering up her real face, when she had now been forced to reveal it. She thought it kind of sad. Tepin had already insisted days before, she do the same for official identity photographs. She should have trusted him.

April was rushing to complete induction, rather than come back the next day. The heathen was in front of her in the college admissions queue, but April barged her way in to stand beside her.

They did their stuff, and finished within moments of each other. April asked her, "You in?"

The girl looked downhearted and said, "Yup, you?"

April said, "No problemo," and high-fived her. April watched her walk away. Something about her attitude reminded her of somebody, not only her father, she just could not place whom.

April was one of the first to move into Zura Hall for that first semester, and she loved all the Aztec stuff. She got registered and obtained her student ID, and did 'official documents'.

She caught the cheap bus back to Pasadena, and called her father as soon as she debarked, using her old sim card for the last time. He sounded pissed as he picked up, "Yes?"

April exclaimed, "Dad, it's me. I need to see you urgently. I have missed you so much!"

She could hear his mood change at once, and he said, "Thank God you're OK! I am on my way this minute, where are you?"

April waited at the time and bus stop he told her to go to, and a few minutes later he pulled up. She got on the back of the bike, and they headed off. He said, "Where to Hon?"

April cuddled him from behind and replied, "Dad, I don't care, anywhere we can be alone and talk—I have so much to tell you."

Bill pulled into a truck stop he had noticed on the way down. Bikers inhabited the place, but few people were around as midday encroached. They took a table out back, and spoke enthusiastically in staccato bursts, each covering bases as quickly as possible.

There came a pause, and April pulled out her new ID, unsure how her father would react. She laid her documents before him, and his brow furrowed, before lightening in astonishment.

April almost whimpered, "Dad, I had to change my life, please don't hate me. I love the name you gave me, I treasure it, but I had to escape, disappear, become somebody else you have no idea … What almost happened. I'll tell all later, but not here, not now."

Bill appeared awed, and through his fatherly admiration managed to utter, "Well, you've certainly done some growing up in the last three months. I can't but believe that I'm a bit happier about how you turned out than your mother would be."

Others came to sit nearby, and it was time to leave. That evening they crossed through Thousand Oaks on a starless night. This represented a new beginning, according to April's limited understanding of Paganism. The motel in Ventura was a dive, but it was safe, and perfect for them.

They ate take-out pizza and Bill went to the cooler to grab a beer; asking April what she wanted. "You got any San Miguel?"

He stopped mid-stride with his back to her, as if checking that he had heard right. He did not remain frozen for long, but neither did he look back at his daughter. He returned with two opened bottles of Bud, and set one before her. April took a slug, and reached for a cigarette. She was also laying the rest of her cards on the table, and willing her father to react.

Chapter 6

Bill looked at her, before looking inwards and saying, "I had my first beer when I was twelve. By fourteen I was having one, sometimes two, every night on the stoop with my Pappy, as he told me stories about life. Started smoking around then an' all.

"You realize these modern laws, they are only made to control people, those same descendants of them that won the West. I remember the local Deputy used to drink with us some nights, especially after evening church on Sunday. Nowadays, if you ain't twenty-one, they gonna charge you with a crime, an' those that gave you the beer an-all, imbeciles!"

Afterwards, they talked for a long time. April related her escape from her mother's house, but refused to say why until she felt ready to tell it. Bill pressed her, and asked, "He didn't, did he?"

April saw his wrath rising, and shook her head. "No Dad, not that. Leave it for now, I'll tell all when I am ready, OK?"

April glanced at the refrigerator and added as an afterthought, "We may need some more beers before we are done tonight, Dad."

Bill seemed to accept his daughter's unease, and held her tight. April knew she would have to tell him everything before the night was done. Returning to her story, she told him how John helped her, and how she ended up in the doghouse, and later in San Diego.

Bill said, "I'll have to step up several gears to keep up with you. I can't believe you escaped, let alone acquired a new, legal ID, and enrolled in college."

"I got the scholarship through ROTC, so be impressed."

"Army. Why not join the Navy?" April could see he was dead proud of her all the same.

"Because there's no ROTC Navy on campus. How'd your freedom trip go, Dad? I know you haven't told me everything."

Bill drained his bottle and returned with two more, a sure sign that he now accepted her as an adult, if a rather young one. April accepted a second beer, but refused the proffered cigarette. Her father asked her again about what made her leave her mother. What could she say, "Soon Dad please, just tell me what you have been doing, how was the road trip. I will tell all afterwards. Promise."

Bill drew the story out, but April knew he was holding back, keeping the best for last. "It was the last call, everything was riding on the turn of one card. I almost backed out. I would lose everything unless I folded. I noticed the guy imperceptivity brush his thumb along the ridge of his nose, and I knew it was his tell."

"I laid my chips and called. He thought he had won, until I laid my cards. I won, sweetheart. I won big. Very big!"

A large grin split his face, and although April tried, he refused to tell how much, for ages. That was until she determined to tickle him into submission. At last he spoke, "I won several million."

He spoke into her astonishment, "I already paid-off the house, and started a college fund for you. Guess you won't be needing that anymore," he chuckled.

They clinked bottles in conspiratorial understanding, their conversation giddy and light. That was until he said, "So what happened, almost happened. Time's up, spill the beans."

What could she tell him, but the truth? April confessed, told all about Creepo Rupert, and her ex-mother's play. Bill swore, "I'll kill the pair of 'em." April believed he meant it, and that he would.

Bill said, "Why didn't you tell me sooner?"

He was mad, and April said, "Because I knew you would kill them, and probably spend the rest of your life in jail."

Bill was subdued, before grabbing another beer for her, and a bottle of Rebel Yell for himself. He usually started on beer, but loved the Southern whisky so much. April needed the Bud to loosen her jaw, and said, "Sounds silly huh?" This was deepest confession time, and she told him everything … He stopped to kiss her wrist; to banish forever back to hell the scar that remained.

All her heartache and anguish poured from her that night, and Bill held her so firmly, not overly tight, but secure, safe. With time, they came to the present, and April said, "That's why I asked you the question about sex. I wasn't quite sure back then, until I got released from hospital, but you had already left by then."

Bill reacted immediately, and unlike every other adult she had ever known, remembered instantly. He answered her question from months earlier, moments before the rattler bit her. Bill used his sketchpad to draw two circles that overlapped in a small eye.

In one circle he wrote the word 'LOVE,' and in the other he wrote 'SEX'. He drew a line from the small intersection of the rounds, and at the end of it wrote 'TRUE LOVE'. He explained, "Both Sex and Love exist in completely different universes most of the time, let's say like porno versus the way I feel about you.

Chapter 6

They are completely inviolate, and unconnected to one another, except for this one small place I know of as true love."

He looked at April, judging her comprehension before continuing, "True Love is the only place where these two combine, as in marriage. It is a special place, and is like a new vision of the world, which is why in this drawing it looks like an eye. I thought I had this with your Mother, but I was mistaken."

Bill's thoughts trailed off—lost in memories. He topped off his shot glass and smoked cigarette. He offered his daughter one of each, but she declined.

He nodded his head in satisfaction, drained another shot before giving her the final pieces of the puzzle, as if fighting to present this new information to her, against the will of his inner demons.

"When you are truly in love with someone, you only ever think about that person. When we were married, I would sometimes find myself looking at other girls, but I never, ever, thought about having sex with them. I only ever thought about making love with your mother, because she was all I ever wanted."

He stilled, before he said a curious thing, like poetry:
"A Man offers Love for Sex.
A Woman offers Sex for Love.
In the Aye of it;
That is where the two become one whole."

April understood his play on the word eye, and Bill smiled, pleased she understood the double entendre. They talked a little more about the diagram, and its implications. He went on to speak about his life and love.

Bill stopped and looked at April during his personal confession, judging her old enough now to hear the rest.

He glugged down his whiskey, and poured another, leaving the offer open for her to join him. "I know young men and women think about sex a lot more often, and especially if they have never had sex before." He stopped again, but this time looked long and hard at her, his unspoken question floating in the air between them.

April responded, "I am still a virgin, Dad, and I do think about sex a lot, but I don't understand it. It's supposed to be great, but my friend says it hurts a lot. I don't know how the two can be the same thing."

They talked about sex and love. April learned so much from him that night, and determined to remain a virgin, despite her stupid hormones.

That short week was the happiest of her life. They followed Highway 1 up the coast, and spent one day deep-sea fishing. That was a total blast. That night they ended up near Monterey, and April chose to drink beer and smoke cigarettes, but only a couple of each. Bill had let her take the big bike a few times on lonesome roads, and she loved it. The powerful motorcycle brought a sense of total freedom she could relate too, and she wanted more. The Harley seemed to throb in tune with her growing adulthood and sexual awareness.

That night Bill let her take him home, and she dropped him at the motel before heading off to get something hot to eat. The only nearby joint still open was a low-class burger bar, but it was cheap and served good portions. She came out and froze. There was a cop looking at the bike, except she knew he was no cop at all. There was something wrong about the guy.

She instantly walked the other way, ducking behind cover, and peering around to observe. He appeared to be calling in a spot check, but he used a head-mic, not a cop radio. The conversation appeared to end when he shrugged his shoulders, and giving the bike one backward glance, strutted off away from her.

April followed at distance, and peering around the corner, was just in time to see him get into the passenger seat of a black V8—like the ones that agencies use on TV. Not Good. The brake lights came on as the motor fired, and she walked back and past her father's bike. She heard the vehicle break out of the side street and watched as it passed her, headed for where the rich lived.

April ran back and gunned the bike, sometimes using the headlight, and sometimes not. She tracked them to a lair set deep within an area of expansive and incredibly expensive mansions. The hoods turned into one that was more like a fortress. April turned the bike around and let it throb slowly downhill in third gear, away from the place. Once clear, she pulled back on the throttle, and boy, did that thing fly. Reaching town she didn't go straight, but knew she had not been followed. She was just enjoying the wind in her hair, and freedom.

She parked the bike in a corner of the yard, and found her father asleep on the sofa, half undressed. The fries were inedible, and the buns, toast. She tried a burger on its own, but it had more cardboard in it than meat. Disgusted, she threw the whole lot in the trash, and went to bed.

Bill woke her with fresh burgers and fries. April filled her father in on what had happened, and he swore. Twenty minutes later, she noticed the same guy was again inspecting the Harley. This time he was dressed in a gangsta-style suit. She told her father and he peered around the drapes, telling her to know your enemy. Bill recognized the guy from somewhere, but when she asked he stated, "Best you don't know, Hon."

April pressed him for an answer, "That guy used to be a mercenary and wanted me to join his outfit. I did not like the people he worked for, and we fell out. That fortress you followed them to must be where the boss hangs out. I never could find it, thanks. Shona, April sorry, that is all I am saying, leave it at that."

They left a couple of minutes later by the rear window, Bill showing her how to loop a cord to close the window properly from the outside. It worked perfectly.

They ran and hid, just in time as the pretend gangsta came around back and checked the window they had just escaped from, before putting his hand to his ear and intermittently speaking to himself. They overheard one side of the conversation, before the hood checked his pistol, and cocking it, headed back around front.

April watched her father put his .38 Special away, and knew that if she had not been there, he would have walked out and confronted, killed the moron.

They followed a decrepit, overgrown path through the rear, and escaped over a small wooden fence. The truck stop nearby was inhabited by pond scum. Bill paid for a ride to Anaheim, and handed her a wad of cash as he left. She noticed him checking his 3-5-7 Magnum before he returned for his Bike. April knew that particular gun had an extra chamber, *Punk*.

They hadn't gone ten miles when the trucker pulled over and tried to rape her—"What is it about men and sex?"

April kicked him hard where it hurt most, took her father's cash back, and was gone. As she watched his dust, she said aloud, "I need a Colt too, even one chamber will do … bring it on."

April made her own way back home; she had learned to rely only upon herself.

Chapter 7 – Confessions

Instead of studying for her high school exams, April found herself studying at San Diego State University. It was hard work, but she had an excellent memory, which helped cover for her lack of education. April knew her core skills were more than adequate for high school but kind of shaky for college, so she signed up for what they called Developmental English and Math.

They were remedial classes for those who hadn't got the grades, the dumbos. She walked in and saw the heathen girl sitting near the back. She thought of sitting by her, but knew her education was much more important than trying to make friends. She sat right at the front, and was the only one that did.

She kept herself to herself in Zura Hall, spending most of her time alone in her room, trying to cope with the mountain of work she was expected to complete. The pressure mounted, and she had to prioritize the stuff she was good at, from the stuff she was not.

Her grades improved afterwards in some fields, and, thanks to her photographic memory, she was catching up with her peers. Many students chose to socialize instead of work on their projects. She hated meeting new people and messing around—pointless. April was doing OK, until the house ganged up on her and would not let her be until she agreed to go to the stupid Halloween party.

April went, but it was mega-boring. People were drinking and being stupid. Most of the water and juice bottles people had smuggled in contained liquor. She got talking to a group of girls, but they only seemed interested in boys.

As if on cue, a couple of jocks came over and started hitting on them. April made to leave, but one cornered her and pressed her to date him. She was not interested in him at all. One of the girls handed April a glass, encouraging her to drink. They seemed OK at first, and April started to relax, until her mind skewed. She knew it was a fix, and she ran. She went straight back to her room, locked and bolted the door, and stuck a chair under the handle. She knew she had been drugged, and crashed onto her bed fully clothed.

After that night, April never again accepted anything from anyone she did not know well. She needed to be able to protect herself, so she joined the campus Kung Fu club. She had gained junior belts before her mother left her father, but with their ever-changing lifestyle, it proved impossible for her to continue.

April joined the campus Wing Chun club through ROTC, who were supportive, and with a special dispensation, paid for full training. It also got her out of some of the Army activities she would otherwise have been committed to attend.

She was early for her first class, and practiced on battering the wooden dummy, or *mook gerk jong*, what they call the post thing with lumps of wood coming out of it. She was so into the flow of repetitive movements, Gary the instructor had to tap her on the shoulder and duck quickly to tell her training was beginning.

She apologized and turned around, only to see the heathen girl standing nearby, giving her a strange look. Their eyes met, but Gary interrupted their 'art of seeing', and said loudly, "Good, I am glad you two know each other, you will make perfect training partners. Please show me your current level."

He stood back and watched as April walked over to join the girl on the mat. She said, "I'm April, you got a name?"

"Annaliese, what's it to you?"

Annaliese held out her hand, as if to shake, and she threw April, who landed on her back. April was slightly winded, but knew she had to rise immediately. The girl was already above her and again held out her hand. "Sorry, that was unfair."

April took her hand to help her up, but threw the girl onto her back, and said, "Think nothing of it, biotch."

After introductions were complete, they squared off properly. Annaliese was a bit bigger and slightly more advanced, but April was quicker and more agile. They were well matched.

They were both oddballs. April liked Annaliese, and soon got back into the routine, taking extra classes when she could. She spending hours deep in thought, or beating the wooden dummy into submission, often doing both at the same time.

Gary called them together one evening, and said, "Girls, I admire your dedication and skills, you are both progressing extremely quickly. Annaliese, I want to postpone your Black Belt by a week, so April to take it with you. Once you are both at the same level, you will both improve much faster in the future.

"Practice the *Wing Chun* forms we will be testing you on, but together—I still remember how you introduced yourselves to each other, and that was impressive. Not for your skills, but for the intensity of your commitment. April, you need to perfect *Nian shou* or sticky hand, and I'll give you extra coaching if you want it.

"You, Annaliese, need somebody who can push you all the way, all the time. Trust me, you will both come on much quicker once you are evenly matched."

Annaliese was disappointed, but saw the logic, as April seldom pushed her to the limit. Their worlds changed from that moment. They each got their First Black Belt, and often went down to practice together in the weeks that followed. They began to socialize after workout.

Over time, Annaliese became a close friend, but April knew absolutely nothing of importance about her life before they met. Annaliese accepted the same from her. Their personal mysteries deepened, but they were two peas in a pod. April concluded 'Liese' was on the run like she was, and probably underage also.

This was highlighted after their next *Wing Chun* examination, which they needed to pass before taking the next belt. The annual break for Thanksgiving was upon them and everyone was going home, but April had nowhere to go, and neither did her friend.

Annaliese

The two girls went back to Annaliese's dorm that night. She bought pizza, while April got a cheap bottle of red wine and a pack of cigarettes. Annaliese remained troubled and broke down, later she told April about her rape.

"It was just before Thanksgiving, some years back. I … I had been to visit my best friend, and we were up in her bedroom talking about music and practicing dance routines, talking clothes and school. Boys I guess. We were both worried that we were fat, but she was thin as a rake. So was I, truth be known, but that didn't stop us dieting. The other girls always looked so thin.

"Her mother interrupted us by asking, 'Claire, can you baste the turkey every half hour, and turn the heat down in an hour? Thanks. Your father is taking me shopping this afternoon, and it will be your fault if dinner is burnt'.

"Her elder brother, Matt, was home, and he called us through to his room, where we listened to music. His friends were nice to us, and offered us draws on a cigarette they were sharing. They all took some pills and washed them down with a glug of whiskey. They insisted we try, and all I remember is the pill was white and had a crown on it. We refused the whiskey, but one of them, the eldest, offered us some cola, which we washed the pills down with.

"He told us to keep the cola, which we sipped from as they continued to talk about stuff. He thought something was funny, and started showing the others porno on his Smartphone. They wanted us to watch, but we left right away. It was gross.

"A bit later, the guys left, the eldest offering Claire's brother a lift in his car. I thought he would refuse, because he was meeting his girlfriend who lived close by, but he got in and they left.

"Matt reminded Claire to baste the turkey, and as they headed out of the door, we went downstairs to the kitchen. A few minutes later, the doorbell rang. It was the older boy who said, 'Sorry, I left my cell in Matt's room. I won't be a second, don't worry, I know the way. Make sure the turkey is basted properly.'

"It seemed like only seconds later when we heard the guy shout from the hallway, 'Thanks, got it.' The front door slammed shut, and when we finished basting. We went back up to Claire's room. April, I know we should have checked, got the cell for him, but we were young and trusted him."

April was quick to speak, "Don't blame yourself, you were a preteen back then. All you did was take some E. End of story. Here, let me give you a hug."

Annaliese pulled away. April realized there was more, and soothed her friend so she could continue. As if a dam had broken within, Annaliese spat out, "That bastard had rufied us April! He must have slammed the front door, but hidden in the house. We began feeling unwell. The next thing was he was with us in Claire's bedroom, his friends taunting us from behind him.

"They were all horny as hell, and ... April, I am not going to tell you what happened next, but we both got raped, plus they made us do other gross stuff. We were gang raped!

"April, to this day, my memory is pretty vague. I do remember the older guy putting a knife at my throat and saying, 'Tell anybody about this and I will kill you.' The only other thing I clearly remember is the smell of burnt, roast turkey at Thanksgiving. To me, that word is a sick joke."

April held her close and it seemed to help. She could not imagine how Annaliese must have felt, or even how she endured. April was aware her fate could have been parallel, but she had escaped. Perhaps they were not so similar after all?

April handed her some tissues, and Annaliese quieted to finish. "We did not know at the time, but the morons recorded everything, and it passed around school like wildfire. I was called a slut and a whore, but I needed help, and there was nobody to talk to.

"Like everybody else, we'd posted on several social media websites, and it only took a day for the cyber bullying to begin. The pictures and video followed, and stills of us apparently getting off on it, they must have been 'Shopped'. The Sickos' even made up a profile about Claire, without her knowledge, showing all the gross stuff, and having her write she was gagging for another session. They posted her cell number and email address. She was bombarded with taunts, and messages asking for dates.

"They did the same with me, phony website and social media stuff, but it wasn't so bad for me because I didn't have a cell or email, but we both had 'chat'. Claire got so upset and ashamed, she cut herself so bad she ended up in hospital.

"I told her to stop visiting the websites, but it was like she was bewitched, addicted with macabre fascination. I was not allowed much internet access at home, and immediately closed all my accounts. Because I wasn't allowed a cell phone, I got off lightly, compared to her.

"I wanted to tell the police, but knew the guy who did it to us would kill me. Now I realise that was just an empty threat to shut me up, let him get away with rape... raping us; raping me.

"If I had my time again, I would call the cops. I would let the police mop up all the semen samples for absolute proof. Same in the hospital for DNA samples, and get blood work to show we had been rufied. Perhaps then things may have turned out different.

"We were scared stiff about our parents finding out. I knew I would be beaten. So we endured the snide comments and name-calling, kids made up stories about us, and blamed us for stuff they did. It seemed every time we were between classes, boys were trying to grope us and pull up our skirts.

"In class, they would slump down in their seats and try to get a view. I covered my legs and knees with a tracksuit top; my parents insisted I wear the school uniform. They called us names like 'fat sluts', which made us both mad at the time, but left us feeling even more insecure afterwards.

"Sometimes boys wanting to get it on stopped us outside school. Gross. We got wise to them. That's when I decided to learn

Kung Fu. I thought my parents would be pleased, but they forbade it, and that always struck me as strange. I now realize they were controlling me, and didn't want me able to fight back against them. I got instruction regardless, using a variety of ruses. Fortunately, they never checked up on me, other than a summary phone call.

"Claire was still addicted to the online media, and tried to fight it, but only ended up dragged in further. One hoax blog turned out to be run by a girl at school who was doing it for a giggle. It wasn't funny. I had dumped all my social media stuff, which is probably why I seemed to handle it better than she did..."

Annaliese drifted into her own mind, as April tried to soothe her. Seeming to realise where she was once more, and what she was doing, revealing, Annaliese continued for completion. "I was too scared, too young, to know all that back then. Is that a crime?

"Claire got me into drugs, which kinda helped, until I came down, then things were worse. The crap of our real lives never went away. It wasn't a way out, but we did it all the same, if only to make the moment more bearable.

"I probably would have become a junkie, but I took some dodgy stuff that made me really ill. I wised-up, and seldom did it after that. I realized the drugs only made things worse. Claire didn't and got into it big time. She even did 'sniff'—glue, thinners, whatever she could get a buzz off. That's when she stopped eating and became anorexic.

"I also had another edge, I realised all the dieting, the outfits, and make-up, were all done to ultimately attract boys. I knew what they wanted, and worked on looking unattractive, repulsive to any man. Claire couldn't see it, she was still competing with other girls. She thought being thin would grant her acceptance.

"Somehow a teacher got hold of the video, and he called the cops, although knowing the perv, I bet he copied it first. The detectives interrogated me as if I was the guilty person, trying to twist my words and get me to admit I was an underage hooker. That hurts, as it was visibly clear we were both rufied, pinned down by much older boys, and raped repeatedly.

"The cops forced each of us to watch the recording, and made us describe what was happening to us. Seeing it again was the last thing either of us needed, it was vile.

"One interrogator kept repeating a gross scene, one where they were forcing me to do a couple of them, so I kept schtum. I cried. I never said another word, or looked up, until a female officer came in. She was as bad, asking me how much money I made. Imbecile! That's the cops for you April, prosecute the innocent, the victims, and let the guilty go free."

April said, "I know, not how you do, but I know the cops' games all too well, and how they try to trick you into saying something in adult words, something you did not mean."

April held her closer, knowing her story was not done. Annaliese confided, "Thanks April, I knew from the moment I first saw you, I could trust you. But it's just so hard, you know."

April

Once finished and calmer, Annaliese looked at her friend, with eyes pleading for greater understanding. April told her some things about her own life, and blurted out, "I also got rufied, last Halloween. The kids on my hall forced me to go, and one jock was sexually aggressive. He kept trying to cop a feel, and I was pissed, Liese. I wanted to flatten him, but it had been a while since I'd gone to Kung Fu training. He was so tall, and big around.

"I accepted a juice from a girl, and tasted a little vodka in it, but there was not much, and I quite liked the flavor. Next thing I knew, my world skewed slightly. I knew they had set me up, doctored my drink, and I had little time left to get away.

"Had I been enjoying myself, I doubt I would have noticed, and probably ended up like you. Here. Let me give you a cuddle."

They hugged, before Annaliese broke away, knowing her friend had also been through shit. Annaliese encouraged April to finish the tale. Needing a distraction to calm herself, April opened the wine, and toasted her friend, before continuing.

"I moved away, as the girl, Shirl I think, was all smiles and asked, 'You OK Hon, you don't look too good'. She was laughing in my face, and I hit her, breaking her nose. Her gallant jock grabbed me by the arm and swung me round. I used the momentum to kick him under the chin. Had I been sober, I would have broken his jaw, but as it was, he staggered backwards and crashed into other people, sending them flying in the process. I ran, and did not stop running until I got back to my room."

As far as it went, April never dropped a hesitation in her soliloquy. They made out that night and it was a simple sharing of the deepest unspoken needs. Neither of them were dykes, but they were both riven by compulsive neediness—to seek solace in each other's arms during times of deepest, most abysmal heartache.

The next morning April bought a burner cell and called Rosa. At first, she was delighted April would visit, but was unsettled that she wanted to include her friend. April explained briefly Annaliese was perhaps more fractured than she had been, asking Rosa for both her indulgence and assistance.

Rosa and her culture didn't do Thanksgiving, so Annaliese would be safe from the smell of turkey. It proved to be a great, long weekend away from being institutionalized. April introduced Rosa as her mother, something everybody found quite funny, but accepted at face value. Later, just before they caught the bus back to town, Rosa said, "Chiquita, Annaliese is a wise choice of friend for you. You are both welcome back anytime."

Christmas and New Year were a trash-liner. The girls stayed and studied most of the time, but did do some ROTC stuff that turned out to be quite good. At least the ROTC consisted of real people, unlike the majority of their peers.

April cooked Christmas dinner, Mexican style. It was hot and feisty. They got drunk and ended up in bed together, again.

Before campus got going again, they started aiming for their Second Dan. April had been hoping her father would show, but he was well off the grid, once more. She got a blank postcard from Seattle, so presumed he was doing OK.

The time was well spent. Not only did they both get their Second Dan, but April also started scoring her first ever 3.0s and got 2.9 overall for her first semester. She became midstream, so no one was bothering with her as an individual.

Annaliese and she both dropped developmental classes, as they were not dumb, but too young, and in April's case anyway, lacked four years of education. She knew that if she had arrived at college five years into the future, as was the family expectation, she would be carrying a 4.0, but as it stood, she was in high spirits. Her new identity was fixed, and she felt settled and secure.

The final exams were a nightmare period. April managed a 3.1 overall for her first year, but she knew it was a close call. Annaliese left immediately after her final was finished, kissed her goodbye, telling April not to worry about her. April knew her friend was up to something, but she wanted to fix it, alone.

Chapter 8 – There But for Fortune

April had decided to head back to Rosa's when a package came. It was from her father, and contained a disposable cell. She knew they would meet soon, something she quickly confirmed. April packed a bag and was waiting for her father's call for a rendezvous, when the TV showed a weird newsflash from Delaware. Apparently, there had been an attack on a suburban home. She was distracted, but was sure she caught a glimpse of someone that looked a lot like Annaliese at the back of the crowd, with a great big smile upon her face.

The police were apparently looking for a 'Lianne Bruer', the family's runaway daughter, to rule her out of their enquiries. It seemed that somebody had disabled the alarm and turned the gas knobs on full, sometime before a Molotov cocktail was hurled into the living room at 2 a.m. The parents were sleeping upstairs and died in the fire. The report mentioned that the daughter had been missing for eighteen months.

April was thinking about this and the wider implications, wondering if she now knew whom Annaliese, or 'Liese', Braun, was.

She was so engrossed in her thoughts and suspicions, she missed the beginning of the next newsflash. Distracted, she heard the name Sally Waverly. April looked up instantly, all senses aware, and saw her ex-mother being bailed for procuring minors. She was indicted on child rape and human trafficking charges. April knew the bitch would be sent down for a long time, and she deserved it.

Bill called at that moment, "You watching the news?"

"Yes, and she deserves it, the cow…"

They talked about her ex-mother for a while, until Bill came to the reason why he sent the burner cell through, "I've come down to LA for a few days, and would love to drop by Aztec, you fancy a vacation in Seattle, Hon?"

April met her father early the next morning, downtown at their usual place. He looked slightly older, but a lot happier. April guessed she looked the same. Once her father's business was concluded, they headed north for his new pad in Seattle, which apart from being a little chilly in winter was a great place, or so he said. She trusted him, and looked forward to the lovely summer sun when they arrived.

They stopped en route, after picking up a slow puncture to the rear tire as they headed for Bakersfield. Bill had the kit to repair it, including a small inflation device, and they were soon on their way once more.

After the early summer heat of San Diego, Seattle was cool and fresh. April liked the layout of the city, and her father showed her around before they went back to his digs. He left the bike in a lock-up, and they walked ten minutes into Rainier Drive, a low-life part of town.

"Being 'off the grid'," he explained, "To me means paying cash, and keeping below any official radar. The place we are headed for is a dump, but it is cash only, and nobody wants to know anybody's business. I'm not even signed in under my real name, so please call me Henry if we run into any kind of trouble, and pretend you are a hooker, or whatever."

They laughed for ages, but April was learning a lot about real life, and a real America few people even knew existed. Bill's hands were stuffed into the pockets of his jeans, and April wrapped both her arms around one of them. It felt mighty good to her, and their adventures 'up north' were only just beginning.

They only stayed in the room he leased for the first night. The next morning Bill rented an RV, and they headed out into the wilds of Washington State.

At first they went east, and then north, following the Columbia River. They lost themselves within the rivers and hills northwest of Wentachee and Lincoln Rock State Park. Bill showed her how to hunt wild animals, and how to make a fire with sticks, without modern aids. April thought that was awesome! They cooked under the stars that night, and the next day he bought her a Leatherman of her choosing.

After a few days, they returned to the city, but went west to La Push to catch Salmon. They caught enough to barbeque and share with others, but doing it once was enough for April. Deep-sea fishing the next day was more her thing, and again they were lucky to get a good catch.

Bill

Bill said, "Now this is what I call freedom. No plans, do what you want to do. Where shall we go today?"

"I wanna ride a horse, and shoot something for dinner."

Those weeks passed so quickly, and felt more like a month. There was a rock concert advertised in Tacoma that Bill desperately wanted to see. He wanted to show April what real music was like. They headed back to Seattle proper, and stopped overnight at Camp Thunderbird, just outside Olympia.

It was close to the city proper, but too touristy for them. The next morning they found a trail and took the camper as far as they were allowed. Bill got the Harley off the back carrier, and they went much farther into the wilderness using forest trails.

At a remote scenic spot with parking, they were donning their stuff for a short hike, when April spotted a car over to one corner. It was the only other vehicle there but she recognized it at once. "Dad...? That's Rupert's car!", and went to investigate.

Even though the plates had been switched, one look inside and April knew for sure. She stated, "I feel like waiting and killing the creep." Bill was about to reply, when they heard a young woman scream nearby.

They ran in the direction of the voice, but it was a lot farther than they imagined. The scream for help came again, much closer this time. Bill dove through a thicket with his daughter right behind him, and came to a small clearing. They saw a young girl, her clothing almost ripped away, trying to fight off a much larger and older man. Rupert.

Bill said, "Wait here, he knows you. I will settle this and save the girl. Take my backpack. Do not follow me, you understand?"

April looked up to follow him, and saw the girl bite Rupert's hand, and Creepo hit her hard. She passed out. The sick bastard ripped her panties away, and began to spread her legs. April was on her feet at once, but ducked down behind cover when she saw her father close quickly on him. She was torn between her father's order, and her will for personal revenge.

Bill was on him before Rupert even knew what hit him, kicking him hard in the face. Rupert parried, and rolled away. Bill thought he would be out cold, but Rupert came to his knees, and drew a pistol. Bill dove as he fired, almost catching a bullet.

Bill rolled and came to a crouch, feinted left, and sprang right. Rupert fired again. The girl came round, screamed again, grabbed

Chapter 8

her clothes, and ran. Rupert's shot missed by a mile, and Bill
pulled his Magnum in earnest. One shot to the heart was all it took.

April

April was there at once, to enjoy watching the pervert's death
throes. It was happening too slowly for her. Her father's shot to the
heart was fatal, but it would take a while. She reached for his gun,
but he said, "Do this, and you will have blood on your hands,
forever. Taking another man's life is not an easy thing to do."

April looked up into his eyes and replied, "That may be so. But
this creep is not a man."

She took her father's Magnum, and shot Rupert square in the
forehead. She hoped his last image of life, was of her, just before
she executed him.

"They say, 'Payback is a Bitch'," but April mused aloud, "That
depends upon your personal point of view. For me, I am that
'bitch', and to me it feels mighty cleansing."

April looked down at the dead eyes, knowing she had ended
Creepo's life. He would have died anyway, but doing it herself was
important to her. She knew her father understood, because he
patted her on the shoulder, before taking his gun back and wiping
it clean.

April looked up at him, with jubilation in her eyes, and a
second later was trying to stop herself from crying. She was riven
inside by the strongest and most conflicting of emotions.

Bill broke the spell by saying, "April, focus. We need to find
the girl, and quickly."

They followed the direction the girl headed in, and coming to
open ground, saw her running for dear life half a mile down the
trail. Bill turned to his daughter and said, "I'll call this in and get
search and rescue to find her. It is not safe in these parts for a child
so young to be alone."

April thought he meant from people, but he added, "There are
bears and mountain lion hereabouts, and she would be a tasty
morsel. Hurry, there is not much time to finish up."

As they ran back to the dead man, Bill said, "Take these keys
and go back to the RV. Return it to the rental yard after you have
thoroughly cleaned out the inside. Then add a little trash, but with
other people's prints, understand? Clean out the inside, but leave
the outside.

"Take both our traveling bags, plus anything you left at my room. You can jimmy the fire escape window easily with your Leatherman, and close it again like I showed you back in Ventura. Head for the Setting Sun Hotel near the docks, and I'll join you as soon as I can. Understood?"

They came to Rupert's body, and April took one final look at the pervert. Her father said, "There's just one more thing. I need you to shoot me."

April spun round on the spot, and he scrunched up his sleeve to reveal a slight graze. Looking her full in the eye he said, "The cops won't think this justification for killing somebody. Hon, I need you to use Rupert's gun, and shoot me in the arm from about five feet away; I know you can do it."

April's world crashed around her as he spoke, but she saw the logic of what he was proposing. How could she shoot the one person she loved above all others, it was crazy. She was frozen to the spot as Bill took Rupert's gun using his kerchief, and handed the covered weapon to her.

Bill walked back to the spot where Rupert first fired at him, and pointed to a spot on the inside his left arm, just above the elbow. He used spit to make a spot for April to aim at, and held the sleeve in place next to his torso. It was barely three-inches from his heart.

April protested, "I can't do this. Why can't we just dump the body somewhere?"

Bill replied, "Because somebody will find it for sure, and when they do, CSI will find a bullet from my gun in his chest, and a second inside his head. I have to call the cops, just as soon as you are out of here. Not just for that poor girl, but for this as well. You got that?"

Her father bade her kneel where Rupert fired from, and encouraged her to be calm and get her mind focused, before she took aim. Somehow, April found a small place of calm within, and remembering her firearms training from ROTC, aligned the sights and pulled the trigger. She wanted this over and done with as quickly as possible.

She threw the gun down and ran to him, his arm was bleeding badly and she went to help him. She was so relieved her aim was true.

Chapter 8

Bill said through gritted teeth, "Damn but that hurts. Excellent shot April. I need to copy what I did before, so the cops can follow the blood trail. Go, people will soon be arriving, if they are not already on their way."

There was no use arguing with him when his mind was made up. He pulled out his normal cell, and called 911. April ran, taking their bags. She made it back to where they left the camper, and got the hell out of there. She was back near the rental yard before she pulled over and took five-minutes out to try and get her shit together.

She drew on a smoke, before she cleaned the RV and returned it twenty minutes later. April made it back to the apartment, and cleared out all her stuff. She took her father's traveling pack as well, and walked for ten minutes before hailing a cab. The Setting Sun Hotel looked worse than his digs, but they asked no questions, and she signed in under a false name.

Chapter 9 – Murder Charge

Up in the room she worried about her father, and felt so helpless, but what could she do? She went out for food, and came back with smokes and a clutch of beers.

April was expecting the cops to keep her father for several days, like last time. However, he called late afternoon and said, "Hon, it wasn't too bad, and I've already been processed and released on bail. I have to go to the hospital for the wound to be re-dressed, but it is already healing. How're you doing?"

They caught up properly an hour later, and Bill told her what went down. "I'm so glad you got clean away, that was my major worry. The Forest Rangers arrived within minutes, and I briefly explained what happened, before showing them where I last saw the girl.

"One of them said, 'Shit! That's cougar country.'

"It was obvious their 4x4 couldn't follow the steep and rough, downhill trial, and they told me the way around would take ages. Against my better judgment, I threw them the keys for the bike, telling them not to put a scratch on it.

"The local Sheriff arrived some time later, accompanied by a team of their finest. I explained what happened, and the man thanked me. I knew I was in trouble, but like me, his concern lay more with the missing girl, than with my actions.

"The mood lightened a few minutes later, when the Forest Rangers called in. They had discovered the girl not far from where we last saw her, and she was fine, although being stalked by a hungry cougar. She confirmed my story about the abduction and attempted rape. That's when the Sheriff shook my hand and slapped me on the back, and I knew everything would be OK.

"We, you and I, did a mighty fine thing today. I am extremely proud of you."

April cut him short, and said, "Why? We only did what anybody else would have done."

Knowingly, Bill shook his head and revealed, "That is not the way of the world. Most people either run and hide, or say they saw nothing. You responded immediately to a cry for help.

"To my mind, a person is not judged by how wealthy, self-important, or high their social rank. They are judged by their actions—whether they lie or tell the truth. If they cheat or offer voluntary aide, and whether they knowingly steal what does not belong to them, or make personal sacrifices to assist those who have been wronged. I call this personal honor."

His words were perfect, and mirrored today's situation. April nodded her head in full understanding and looked at him. Her father winked back at her, and said, "Fancy a cold one Hon?"

He had brought back a bottle of Rebel Yell, and cold San Miguel for his daughter. April clinked her bottle with his tumbler, and they drank to their own good health, and Rupert's death.

April tried to ask him about the wound, but he dismissed her inquiry, saying, "Later, it is nothing. Let me finish telling this story first. The bullet wound so close to my heart was key, thank you sweetheart, I know that was tough on you."

April said, "You bet it was, what if I had missed by three inches. You would now be dead!"

She was on the verge of throwing a childish tantrum, when Bill concluded. "But you didn't miss. Your hit was a bull's eye, and well you know it. Congratulations. Not many Marines would take that particular shot, but you did. Respect where respect is due."

He held April close, and her phony upset was replaced by something much deeper, a mixture of love, reverence, and admiration. It was a complex feeling, and almost as baffling as being highly praised—April had never been any good at receiving compliments, which she normally dismissed as people being ingratiatingly silly.

That night, she was moody and could not settle. The TV was annoying and disrupted her thoughts. Every channel was reporting on the attempted rape of a minor, and the killing of Creepo. Bill was being hailed by the media as a hero, which April already knew he was. He had always been her hero, so she paid it little mind. She felt both proud and satisfied. She had kept the promise she made to herself, and killed Creepo Rupert. She saw it not so much as murder, but rather done in the way someone would dispatch a rabid dog.

This was entirely at odds with the torment of having taken the life of another human being. OK, he would have died a minute or two later. Regardless, she pulled the trigger that snuffed out his miserable existence. Like her father had said at the time, now she had to live with it.

April wanted to cry for the life she had taken, but how could she? The only thing she had actually stolen was his chance for redemption, and she did not in the least believe he would have availed himself of that. The tears would not come. Justice had been served. Bill held her tight as she let it all come out. It was a further cleansing of sorts. He told her, as she settled into his heartfelt embrace, that if she had not shot the bastard in the forehead, then he would have done so. April almost felt whole once more. The world of grownups and their complex emotions was becoming so confusing.

April fell asleep in her father's strong and comforting arms, and woke refreshed. In her waking moments, thoughts of death and rape flittered up from her subconscious, but she swatted them away like annoying flies in the heat of summer. She got straight out of bed, and strode purposefully forward to meet the new day on her own terms.

She was unaware, but must have been woken by the sound of a telephone ringing. Her father was speaking into his regular cell, and she heard him say, "Yes Sheriff, I'll be there as soon as I can … I'm so glad she's OK and wants to see me, although I was only doing what anyone could have done."

The call ended and he looked over at his daughter, adding, "The Sheriff is holding a press conference this morning, all official like. The Mayor will be there, and he wants to be seen on camera with me and the girl we saved. I think it is all a part of his re-election campaign, but if it gets me off the hook for murder, then I'm gonna take it."

He rushed to get ready, calling out, "Do I need a suit?"

April scolded him, "What? This from the man who's always telling me to be myself, live my own life. I can't believe you just said that."

Bill chuckled knowing she was right. He looked at her as he went to leave, and said, "Don't get into any more trouble while I am gone. Love you!"

He did the hand gesture as usual, and she pointed back at him saying, "You."

April felt the emptiness as soon as he was gone. She needed action, anything to keep her mind busy, breakfast, coffee at least. She had always drunk orange juice early in the morning, but these last few days she had tried her father's coffee, and had grown to like it strong and sweet, with far too much milk. He took it black.

Wandering the local streets in a bad part of town, she could not get over how different and safe the city felt, from virtually the rest of the U.S. The best parts of LA seemed more threatening to her than this, one of the worst parts of Seattle.

She meandered around and began to learn the nearby streets; there was nothing else for her to do. She came across an information wall near one of the pedestrian entrances to the docks proper, and saw ads for coast-hopping crew. The deal was free passage for free work. She snapped a picture with her Smartphone, and walked away, not sure why she had bothered.

April was bored. She was not into 'shopping' as most other girls were, so she went back to the hotel and slept. She was not tired, but sleeping was better than being awake. She was having a great dream, when her cell rang. It was her father.

"Hon, I'm sick of playing the local hero. I'm headed off to Joe's bar to clear my head. I won't be long, but I fancy talking to real people for a while, and taking the locals on at darts. I would ask you to join me, but we can never be seen together until you are out of this city. Trust me. Later I'll bring food back, what d'you fancy?"

He was late back, but April knew he would be. She understood he needed the personal space—people who wear their heart on their sleeves often do. Regardless, he had been arrested for Murder One, and could spend the rest of his years in jail. Despite her father's flippant air, she worried the case would go against him once the detectives and lawyers got hold of it. Troubled by disconsolate thoughts that seemed to spread alarmingly, she was saved from a black mood by her fathers return.

April had asked for Mexican. He dropped a bag of freshly pickled, hot chilies on the bedcover between where they sat, and said; "Best I could come up with at this time of night."

He threw on top a pack of fresh corn-bread wraps, assorted sliced meats, salad, and got chili sauce, garlic mayo, and pesto out of another carrier; they were in business. It was not Mexican culinary art, but it tasted damn fine as they mixed and matched ingredients to their personal whim or fancy.

A few days later, Bill had to go to court again, as a witness for the defense of the girl involved. She turned out to be a few months younger than April had been when she ran away.

The following day, Bill was back in the same court, facing charges of first-degree murder. When they met later, he told April what had happened, "The murder charge was dismissed immediately, and apparently, the judge called the prosecution counsel *in camera*, to have a serious talk with them.

"The outcome was I was bailed without bond, to attend the next hearing, more than one month away. I am legally bound however, to remain in Washington State for the term before trial.

"Nonetheless, I gotta get you out of here quick. But every traffic cam and cop in the city will be looking out for me. They'll want your ID for the bus, and if anyone works out who you in truth are, we are both in deep shit. I guess we could hire a boat from some secluded marina that asks no questions, although in this city, that is highly unlikely."

As soon as April heard him mention the word boat, she got out her Smartphone and showed him the picture she took of the information wall at the docks. "Could I get away like this?"

Bill looked at her and shook his head despondently, before saying, "No, you could not work your way south, but we can."

A large smile morphed onto his face. "Pack all your stuff now, we leave in five, and will take a ride on our luck. I need to see you safe back to SD, and afterwards, I will come back here to face whatever happens."

They were gone inside of ten minutes. April had to buy her father a hoodie and false beard on the way. He was useless at disguising himself, but they got into the docks proper by joining a group, and headed directly for one of the berths mentioned on the information wall.

Bill removed his disguise as soon as they started canvassing the ships mentioned. At first, they struck out, but one Bosun was interested in them, and later the Captain took them on. Because he knew a lot about ships, Bill was working passage for a little pay, with April earning nothing as the kitchen help. They came out of it a little up, but both of them learned a lot and had a great time.

Bill gave April a Walther PPK/S when they got back to San Diego, with several extra clips and a couple boxes of rounds. He paid extra for Hilcott, an ex-Marine buddy of his, and now a

Chapter 9

licensed firearms dealer, to add a silencer. This meant replacing the original barrel with one that had a screw thread for the muffler.

April asked, "Why don't Walther make a gun barrel with a screw thread? They could also sell the muffler as a package."

"Don't ask me, Hon. Because they're stupid I guess."

Time was short. April knew he needed to get back to Seattle as quickly as possible.

The next day Bill slipped his daughter a small roll of hundred dollar bills for her next year at college, impressed with her first year's efforts. He left at once to crew the same ship back to Seattle, and face his destiny.

Chapter 10 – Rape in the Hood

Back in college, April declared a major in communications and added theater as a minor, which was a lot more in tune with her past education or lack thereof. This time she moved into private digs with Annaliese, where they shared a one-bedroom hovel. But it was their hovel, their freedom, and it suited them well.

The room was in a zero star converted bordello. It had been busted some years back when the city fathers raided once too often, and the Mayor closed it down forever. It was now home to the wealthier down and outs, druggies, harmless sickos, and a few students. Otherwise, its seedy ambience had remained unsullied, as nobody wanted to know anybody else's business. It was similar to the hotel in Seattle, and it suited them just fine.

Everything was okay for the first month, except April worried about her father. When they spoke, he told her everything was 'fine', and she knew he was shielding her from his worries. The legal battle was about the second bullet to Creepo's brain, the one April had put there. The heart shot was clearly self-defense. Apparently, finishing him off moments before he would have died anyway was murder—according to the prosecution.

These worries multiplied as time moved on, but April could do nothing. Neither could she let it go. She tried to call her father, but his cell had been turned off for three days straight, and in desperation, she called John from the same burner cell.

The landline answered and John said, "I am sorry, but you have reached the wrong number. Please refer your unwanted sales scammers to the nearest psychiatrist, and stop hassling me!"

April wanted to laugh, because this was so like him, but she knew he was about to slam the phone down. He did. Ouch! She laughed because some sales morons had obviously gotten hold of his number, and were making his life hell. She called again, and started speaking as soon as he picked up, "April. John, this is April. I need your help, what's happening to Dad?"

The line went quiet for a moment before John said, "Sorry April, was that you calling just now? It's been a nightmare ever since some cowboy 'marketeers' got hold of my unlisted number. Your Father is OK do not worry. Look, right now is quite awkward for me, I'll see you soon and explain all."

Chapter 10

John drove down the next afternoon, and April met him as soon as her last class finished. She got in the passenger seat, and Satan was all over her before she had a chance to close the door. He ended up sitting on her lap, and he was a lot bigger and heavier than she was. John could do nothing but wait until Satan's focus of enthusiasm left her, and he threw a doggie treat onto be back seat.

They spoke about general things, John was avoiding questions about April's father. "April wait, later OK? Now what type of restaurant do you fancy: French, Mexican…?"

She went along with his designs for the evening. He took her to a good restaurant, and later to a beach she did not know about. It was sort of a local hotspot, because there were bars and Latin music all around, they got drinks, and found a quiet spot to talk.

John took a long, slow slug of beer before finally coming to the point of their meeting. Now more relaxed he said, "Bill told me he'd be here himself, except he's still up in Seattle awaiting trial, though he is still out on bail with few conditions.

"However, the City Attorney, the C.A., is now involved, and he wants to prosecute your father to the fullest extent of the law. Meanwhile the Sheriff wants all charges dropped, and the media is on the Sheriff's and your father's side. The Mayor is trying to ride both horses, but will have to side with one or the other. He has already backed your father, right at the beginning, so it will be difficult for him to side with the C.A.

"This is petty politicking in election season Sho…"

April stopped him mid-word and said, "John, please, I use my real name, April. I've given up that baby name and live in dread that someone will hear it and start using it, even in fun. Now tell me, is my Dad OK?"

John picked up where he left off, "April, lovely name, reminds me of spring. That is how I will always think of you. Apologies.

"Regardless, I went up to see Bill last week, and know your father is fine. Here's the crux of the problem. By rights the C.A. would normally get his way, except this is election season. Everyone in office wants to be re-elected on November seventh, that's less than one month away.

"Your father is a hot potato, ricocheting around the political spectrum like a ball released on the handle pull of a pinball machine. The party spin-doctors are having a hard time, because last week a hooker was raped and murdered. The police found her corpse, half eaten by a mountain lion; it was not far from where your father saved that girl.

"Sh—April, know he told me everything. We are extremely close. I hope you have a friend as close as your Father and I are."

John stopped to take a drink of his beer, and April said, "Yes, I do have a friend like that, I think, but only one. Maybe with you, two?"

She looked up at him and he stated, "There is never any 'maybe' about it, not with your truest friends. They accept you for who you are, all your strengths and weaknesses, all your brilliance and stupidly. None of us can ever be perfect, never forget that. But we can try our best to be stout of heart and stand up for what we believe in, and for those more vulnerable."

He looked at her most seriously and added, "I would also have put a bullet through that guy's brain," John spoke conspiratorially, whispering, "Knowing the pair of you as well as I do, I would guess you were also there, and you ended the pervert's life. But that is irrelevant. Well done."

April was devastated, but knew her father had not told him everything, John was perhaps snooping, trying an angle to see if she reacted. Like her goth mask, her poker face remained stalwart. April looked him in the eye and called him out, "I wouldn't know. Stop. Leave now, John, or tell me about my father. And drop the petty snooping, it doesn't become you—that is, if you really are my father's truest friend?"

John was visibly shaken by her abrupt attack. He apologized at once, and came back on track.

"The problem up in Seattle is one of 'right versus wrong'; one of a man's spur of the moment reactions. The defense is stalling for time, since soon the C.A. will start the main thrust of his own re-election campaign, and he certainly will not want to be seen as the villain in this court battle.

"April, I think it safe to say, the Sheriff will be re-elected, and win your father's battle also. As long as the media remain on Bill's side, you both have no worries. I doubt he will even get a warning. Bill is safe so do not worry. He is most worried about you."

They talked, and something John had said made April ask, "What do you know about my mother, how she met dad?"

John almost choked on his beer, before trying to dismiss her question. She pressed until he admitted, "I only knew Sally in

73

Chapter 10

passing in those days, and seldom spoke to her. She called herself Mustang Sally, and was rumored to be a hooker. However, we all knew she helped-out voluntarily at Girl Scouts, so that never made any sense, well, until quite recently.

"April, I do not know if she was on the game, that's just what the word was, OK. She was always hanging around at Marine Corps parties, a good time girl, if you know what I mean.

"She was one of those women attracted to a man in uniform, any man in uniform. The last I saw of her was at Bill's discharge bash, and she only had eyes for him. I tried to intervene when he was alone, but by then, he was under her spell.

"They left early, together. I never saw her again until Bill said she needed a house, and the one down from me was up for sale. I suggested it, if only so I could keep an eye out for you. That was what your father wanted me to do.

"April, I don't know anything more, anything for sure. However, when he caught her running around on him, it did not surprise me. I'm sorry to speak ill of your mother, but I'm just telling it like it was back then. Forgive me."

April smiled ruefully, her eyes dark with deeper knowledge, now confirmed. She was her father's girl, no longer her mother's daughter. She thanked John for his honesty, and needed a distraction.

Satan was bored, and wanted something to do as well. He put his head on April's lap, and looked up enquiringly with mournful eyes. How could she refuse? She needed the break, and went to buy a ball, but ended up with a Frisbee. She threw it and Satan chased, and chased it again on her next throw. He was not too good at bringing it all the way back to her, until she threw it into the sea. They both ended up swimming sometimes, and at other times, having fun in the surf and sand.

John crashed on the floor of their room that night, and before he went to sleep, he told her he had slept in a lot worse places. April woke with Annaliese berating Satan, who had somehow ingratiated his way to sharing their bed. She was not impressed, but April had her arm and leg wrapped around her hero, and felt secure. Satan must have licked Annaliese's face, because she fought the dog's playful advances off, and bolted for a shower. A lone voice from below tried to reanimate, "He needs food and water, give me a minute. Did we really drink so much last night?"

"No, only you did. I had to drive us back, or don't you remember." April had zero sympathy for John, and the girls had fun teasing his awakening. Even so, he treated them all to breakfast, and left for LA a short time later.

A few weeks after, it was Annaliese's birthday, well celebrated in fine style, and the build-up to Thanksgiving. They were preoccupied by a lot of course work, plus some ROTC stuff. Annaliese became a bit moody, but April put it down to the time of the month, before she realized it couldn't be, because they had somehow, almost cycled together.

April looked at the roll her father had given her, and it was a little smaller than she had hoped. She knew her best friend needed a lift, and with time would come her reason. She took a hundred dollar bill, and decided to take her out for the night. Annaliese wasn't having it, so they settled on Mexican takeout and red wine.

They agreed April would get the meal and Annaliese the wine, then April's cell rang. It was John with news from Seattle. She handed Annaliese the note and mouthed, "Dad" at her. Annaliese gave her a thumbs-up, and left indicating she would get the food.

John spoke immediately, "I don't have much time, listen. The new C.A. still wants to press homicide charges against your father, but the reelected Sheriff remains a staunch supporter of Bill. There are many legal arguments, centering mainly around the 'Stand Your Ground' law, and the similar but different 'Castle Doctrine', or the right to 'not retreat'.

"I think Bill may get off scot-free, or with only an official police warning. Nobody knows about you. You've lucked out April. Bill told me to tell you he will be down to see you, just as soon as he can."

"Cool. I'm sure Dad will be OK, thanks. How's Satan enjoying Washington State?"

"I think he's found a new girlfriend. There's a bitch in heat nearby, and you know what that means…"

They laughed and hung up. April skipped out to get the wine, and was looking forward to their meal. She got back and looked at the clock, wondering what was taking her friend so long. Her cell rang. She looked at the caller ID, and it was Annaliese.

April picked up immediately, and heard a scream followed by the sounds of a struggle. The noises were indistinct as if the cell were on the ground. She knew instantly her friend was in deep shit. She was fighting for her life, as a gang of men taunted her for sex.

By the time April found her in the alley they used as a shortcut, Annaliese had laid two of them out, but was held from behind and being stripped naked with a long, sharp blade.

April could never get close enough without a ruse. She paused out of sight to spin on the silencer, arm the pistol, and pulled her hoodie up. She walked like any disinterested teen, and rocked her head as if she was in a world of her own, listening to mp3s. She got close and kept looking at her feet, aware of the slightest movement any of them made. Annaliese was by then unclothed; the hoods' full attention was focused on pawing her. April got past them with only superficial glances in her direction.She whirled, flicking the safety off, and fired at close range.

She took out both goons to either side, and nailed the leader between the eyes as he turned to strike at her with his machete. Annaliese kicked the shin of the guy who was holding her as hard as she could, and threw him, turning her throw to dislocate his arm as he went over. He landed badly on his back and April silenced his pain with a bullet through his eye.

She shot the two Annaliese had already floored for good measure, and stayed to tidy up. Annaliese arranged her tattered clothes so she appeared to be dressed, while April grabbed a plastic bag blowing in the wind, and searched the hoods' wallets. They took most of whatever cash they had, leaving just enough for the cops to exclude robbery as a motive. They where about done when they heard a sound nearby, and fled, taking the Mexican food and Annaliese's cell phone with them.

Once clear, they kept to the darkness and went a long and circuitous way back to their home. They were almost spotted a couple of times, but instead of running, stopped and made-out as young people do in the shadows. April knew she needed the close loving comfort, Annaliese even more so.

April knew, ID aside, she was still only fifteen years old, and had just killed another six men. She felt nothing.

Last summer she had mourned killing a pedophile who had wanted to rape her, and was in the process of raping another innocent. This time she felt the urge to spit upon the rapists' corpses. She had not, if only because of DNA evidence linking them back to the scene. Had she changed, or had life changed her?

April realized both statements were true, and that she was growing up.

When they could talk privately, Annaliese thanked her, but looked at her friend with concern, "April, are you all right?"

April replied, "I have just killed six men, and I feel nothing. Zilch, empty somehow. I killed someone once before, and that affected me a lot, even though he deserved it. Do you think there's something wrong with me? Am I psycho?"

Annaliese grabbed her by the arms, shaking as she spoke, "No, there is nothing wrong with you. I killed a couple of people some time ago, and they had it coming to them. You get hardened to it, Hon. Had this been the other way around, I would have shot all six morons just like you did. Think nothing of it."

Annaliese said she was OK, but April knew she was not. They could not face the food, but did drink the bottles of cheap red. April held Annaliese tight all night and got little sleep herself. Her friend's nightmares had returned, and Annaliese spent most of the night waking and shaking involuntarily within April's arms. She rushed to the bathroom and was sick a couple of times. This gave April time to dwell on her lack of remorse, but she did feel guilty, and was also feeling queasy. She went to comfort Annaliese; the smell of fresh vomit reacted on her own senses, and she threw up, pushing Annaliese out of the way.

The next morning Annaliese assured April she was fine, but April did not believe her. They left for class together, and Annaliese seemed to brighten by the time they reached college. April did her day and texted Annaliese's cell several times, but there was no reply. Worried, she grabbed some street food for the both of them, a couple of bottles of red, and headed back to the room they shared.

April found her friend half-naked, sprawled across the bed. She had an "Ambient" CD playing on repeat, a burned-out candle and cup of foil nearby, and a smelly clay pipe lying idly by the bed.

April knew she was stoned. Annaliese came to a few hours later, her mind a cacophony of myriad thoughts and self-loathing. She disinterestedly ate a few mouthfuls of cold food, and became more human, but said, "I've got the munchies, and needed juice, fast."

Chapter 10

April rushed to the nearest store and bought chocolate, chips, and assorted snacks.

April's mind kept thinking about her friend. She knew the attempted rape from last night had triggered something much deeper within her soul, some wound that could never heal, unless the poison within was exposed and eviscerated.

Annaliese never normally did drugs, but here she was, as fragile as a snowflake in a hurricane. It was clear to see she was trying to stay in the calm center of whirlwind emotions, but that a new storm was ominously approaching, the back-ass of the same one.

April needed to reclaim her friend, before the other side of the rotator manifested. She returned with the treats, and Annaliese wolfed them down. It was just as well April had filled a carrier with her favorites. April waited until she was almost human again, before zooming in on her like a twister.

April coaxed and cocooned Annaliese's fragile self as best she could, but knew this demon, or whatever it was that taunted her, had to be dispelled once and for all. She had put a bottle of Rebel Yell to one side, for if her father ever showed up. April opened it and poured them each a large measure, determined to hear it all, to out the worst her friend always kept hidden secretly inside. Scorpios can be like this, too proud to admit the truth, even to themselves sometimes.

April pressed her by saying, "You are my best friend, and I'd do anything for you, you know that. I cannot let you go on like this. Whatever it is Liese, give it up!"

Annaliese looked back at her and nodded her head, saying, "I will, I promise, in a minute, but not just yet. You got any more of that whiskey?"

Chapter 11 – Sick Society

Time moved on, and it was well after midnight when Annaliese became angry and cried out to April. "Why do men always do that? They are so much into their *'I am going to fuck you so good, and I know how to do it better than any other man'* macho bullshit, that they don't even see the damage they are doing to women—their prey. To all humanity. I hate them."

Somehow, April realized she was not talking about last night, but her first gang rape. Then she remembered that had happened around Thanksgiving, and felt like a dumb schmuck.

She refreshed both tumblers, and called Annaliese out. Her friend was hesitant at first, but April knew her well enough to press the right buttons, and eventually she gave out. It was much worse than April had imagined.

"April, you have no idea how difficult this is for me. If I tell all, will you hate me also?"

April didn't know what her friend was talking about, or why she said it, but the words sort of left her lips without thinking. "I saw something months back on TV, a newsflash of a house explosion in a burb of Delaware. The reporter said the cops were looking for a 'Lianne Bruer'. I'm sure I saw somebody that looked a lot like you at the back of the crowd, but it could never have been you of course. Level with me, if only to share with someone that loves you for whom you are. OK?"

Annaliese looked up into April's eyes like a mouse who had just walked within striking range of a snake. April pressed once more, "Give it up and release it, you need to free yourself of whatever haunts you. My lips are sealed."

Annaliese gulped down the whiskey like Bill would, and topped off both glasses. She took another drink immediately, but it was just a sip, she was battling, a war raging within her heart and mind. She looked at the glass, and looked away from April, who was worried she had pushed her friend too far, but waited her out.

Some seconds later, Annaliese reached for her hand, and April covered it with her other. The girl imperceptibly nodded her head, and said, "I already told you about losing my virginity to my first gang-rape. That was just the beginning…"

79

Chapter 11

She faltered for a moment, took another slug of whiskey, turned her head further away from her friend. Her grip of April's hand became like a vice.

Her words, when they finally flowed were calm and collected, as if she was reporting a routine event for television. There was no emotion in the steady meter of her voice, but the rest of her appeared to be entering a mental abyss. April winced at the pain in her hand, and gripped Annaliese back equally hard.

Annaliese stated detached and coldly, "The police interrogated me as if I was the criminal, and asked me all sorts of leading questions, trying to put words into my mouth. I already told you that.

"I also told you they were desperate to charge me with soliciting underage sex. They seemed intent on putting me on the sexual offenders register as an underage hooker. Get real!"

Annaliese turned her eyes towards her friend, and April could see the unjustness and hurt the cops had caused. Their eyes locked for an instant, before Annaliese glanced away and continued her confession. "What I desperately needed was love and counseling. Instead, I got fuck-all. I was bullied, bailed, and brought back home to my parents. I knew they had been at the police station at the beginning, but left before I was dealt with.

"As soon as I walked in the door, mother called me a slut and spat, 'You made your bed, now lie in it'. She slapped me real hard, before she stormed off in disgust.

"My father hit me hard and said with mounting malice, 'You are no longer my daughter. You manifest the abhorrence of Satan, you have become the Devil's Daughter, his whore. Come, I must cast this evil out of you, so help me God!' He threw me over his knee and beat me with his belt. As the leather scarred, welted, and blooded my butt he preached a seemingly never-ending series of religious paradigms. Held fast, I screamed aloud in pain… until mother gagged me.

"That night the abuse started, my own father using my body most evenings for his personal gratification. April, I was only eleven years old…"

Annaliese trailed off and shook her head, as if trying to rewrite her past, but they both knew what was done would never go away.

It was plain to see, Annaliese hated living, but what could she do? Through no fault of her own, she had been raped. The result being, she had become her father's whore. She admitted to April, "I had to endure my father's abuse every night, alone."

April knew an abominable sore festered deep within her friend's psyche, a stain implanted so regularly, so deeply within her budding body, it demanded eradication—the ultimate cleansing. If she had murdered her parents, then April stood shoulder to shoulder with her. Some of the things people do unto others will always remain: Unforgivable!

Annaliese added distractedly, as her mind continued to mull over the memories no child should ever have. "After that first night, the rape by my father, my parents treated me worse than a dog. Apparently, I had offended their god. They used to be Mormons, but had recently joined some new cult, 'The Brethren of the Flail of Yahweh'. I never could understand that, but I seemed only to live and endure my next beating and nightly father-rapes.

"The only thing they taught me, was that 'god' does not exist. All this religious crap, was only a means for them to control me. You do understand that, don't you April? That's why I'm Heathen. Sure... Sure, I now realize all they were doing was ostracizing me from the world I knew, they isolated me so I could not report them, in order to protect themselves from prosecution. Not me from sexual slavery and daily rape. Sicko's.

"And the Lord God said, 'Reap what you sow'."

April held her close, having finally managed to extract her hand from her friend's fierce grip. "That's when it started... the drugs. They never let me be, you know? No you don't, thank God!

"Before I reached high school, I was snorting Coke for confidence, some Crystal to get me by, but H was the best, when I could get it. I haven't done that in years, until today, but it wasn't the gen stuff you know."

April froze. Annaliese's memories were indistinct, but she latched on to the cult connection, hoping to drag her friend's mind back, clear away from the abyss.

April dramatically changed the subject, going back to what Annaliese had said before. "Religious cults, Huh! So did my mother. First, she joined some snake sect, but after she left Dad, we moved and she joined some quasi-religious cult. I wonder if it was the same Brethren? I thought she lost contact the next time we moved."

Chapter 11

This seemed to open a way forward for Annaliese, who sobbed about how her own parents groomed her for sex, how she was told it was normal, and she was doing vital work for her mother.

April said, "Conditioning," and thought she was done. She moved to put both arms around her companion, but Annaliese shook her head. "There's more."

They both drained their glasses and topped-off. April could not imagine how her friend's life at that point, could get any worse, but Annaliese surprised her by saying, "The harassment at school, the bullying, taunts, and sexual jibes, got so bad Claire and I were forced to change schools. We ended up at different ones.

"At first it was cool, but then somebody recognized me from the video the rapists took, and the whole thing started up all over again. Every day became a repeat of the same nightmare, and every night, my father raped me. I wanted to die.

"Claire and I got together sometimes, and we made a suicide pact. She was heavily into cutting, and it looked so cool, I tried it, and became addicted. The pain was a release, you know. The oozing blood was great, and I played with it, writing signs and symbols on my arm, her arm, we shared and discovered a place in our heads where nobody could hurt us, bully us. I even cut her, and she me, that was a blast!"

"The drugs helped. Sort of made it go away, seem normal, natural. But she always paid too much attention to what anonymous people thought of her and had done some sexting. I told her she was crazy, but she shrugged it off, 'If I don't, they make my life hell at school the next day'. The last time I saw Claire alive, she had made a date with one of the internet hustlers; I talked her out of it, but think she went regardless. It's sad, I was her only true friend in real life.

"After that night, I sort of stopped seeing her, she was bringing me down. It wasn't planned. She just got busy. I got busy trying to start a new life, but I was still living my old one, and that never works. To begin again, you need to start proper, afresh. A clean slate and no reminders of the past."

April said, "You sure do. I had to live somewhere no one would know me, and the goth is my way of making sure. That's why I ended up in SD."

They talked about freedom for a while, until April asked, "How many times did you start over?"

"Too many." Annaliese's focus returned to the story. "It wasn't long before I was forced to leave the new school, and I got a savage beating because of that. You've seen the scars. Did you ever wonder about them? When he had finished lashing my butt and back, father put me in the car, mother put a bag of my belongings in the trunk, and we drove west for five days.

"Eventually we arrived in the northern wilds of Arizona. At first, I thought the place was a small town, since it only had a couple of stores and a church. It turned out to be the headquarters of their cult, and consisted entirely of their community and sect members. I was there to go to their school.

"Father stayed for several days, and gave me away. I was married into the Brethren. That was their scam, and justification to use me as a sex toy; they made the most of it. There was nobody I could trust, and I hated them all.

"In the beginning, I thought about running away, but at eleven, no by then I was twelve years old, how could I? Their cult banned modern tech, they did not allow cell phones, computers, games consoles, or TV. It was like going back into the Stone Age. April, the only contact I had with the outside world was when my parents visited occasionally.

"Every time I objected, or did not do what I was told, I was beaten. Eventually I sort of gave up, and did whatever it was I was told to do, to avoid being hurt any more. I felt like their slave, not a child. I hid behind a public mask, but never bothered to look out from behind it. Nothing ever changed.

"Do you know, April, when you are beaten every day, naked, in front of everyone, you sort of get used to it. The pain, the constant floggings, and the indignity. April, feel my back. Those are callused welts. My hide got strong.

"Just like my father, they'd rant fanatically between every strike of birch or leather against skin, 'I'll teach you the error of your ways'. It was a sort of despotic version of 'I'm only beating you for your own good.'

"When my daily, public flogging was over, they would turn back to the congregation, exclaiming victory over the ungodly to the daughters and wives, preaching—'This is where you end up if you behave thus and worship the Devil.'"

Annaliese was shaking as she relived those moments, and April confessed her own admission of guilt and sorrow, "Liese, remember my mother tried to sell my virginity to a sex slaver, but I found out just before he came to collect me, and I ran away at once. They never did catch up with me."

Up until that point it had felt like there had been a barrier between them. This melted away with April's admission, and Annaliese opened her heart to April, as the last of the tale was spoken, "Then in truth you do understand. You are not just saying that. You believe me?"

April looked at her friend calmly and said with strength of conviction in her voice, "Yes, I believe you one hundred percent. If I had not, by chance, overheard my mother on the telephone, I would be in some child-sex warehouse right now."

Annaliese took comfort from April's strength, and finished quickly, "I hated everybody and everything about my life. I even hated myself for allowing it to continue. I cut myself, a lot, and cried myself to sleep most nights.

"I usually had 'female services' to perform each evening for the ringleader, after the religious cult stuff and evening service to their 'god' was done with. Otherwise, I was locked in my room most of the time. Two years later a new girl arrived, and she became the cult leader's favorite, she was three years younger than I was, do the math.

"I hoped this would set me free, but instead I was passed around the other men there. Sometimes several men would take me as a group, often allowing one of them to film it. Sick. It was still rape, even if I just let them get it over and done with, what choice did I have?

"I wanted to kill myself, and thought about it seriously for a long time. In the end, I said to myself, 'Liese, are you living for the present, or for what has passed already?' I determined to live for the future, and chose to embrace it, no matter what the cost.

"I don't know what would have become of me, if one evening there had not been an outbreak of food poisoning."

April was quick, noting her friends smile, "You didn't, did you?"

Annaliese shrugged, "I found some wild mushrooms and added them surreptitiously to the stew—I hoped to kill us all. It didn't, but it was bad. I was one of the few who got it early, and it did not affect me too badly. I knew what not to eat.

"As one of the few still on their feet, I was sent to the store to call for the doctor. I was alone and called Claire. Instead, her father answered, and when I asked for her, he told me she had committed suicide the year before, and slammed down the phone.

"I was stunned. She had made the ultimate sacrifice to free herself. I stared at the phone, becoming a victim had forced her to give up all hope. I wanted to cry, but was surprised when instead of tears, an old feeling resurfaced after lying dormant for many years. I knew I had to get away and stop being a victim. I had rediscovered the courage to stand up for myself, the need to be free. I rushed out, intending to pack my backpack for school as usual, but not with school work, and disappear."

April interrupted, "I had already packed my school bag and was planning to do the same thing, when the pervs arrived one night early. Wow! This is weird."

Annaliese replied, "It sure is, but I never got that far. There was a pickup truck at the gas pumps, and I knew it was headed off somewhere. It was blue, the color of freedom, I thought. I managed to sneak aboard the back and got to Page, Arizona. My next ride took me west to Vegas, and the third got me to SD. From the moment I got away, I always wanted to kill my parents."

April said, "Me too, not my father of course, but mother and her pervert boyfriend who lived with us. He tried to rape me a few times you know, but I used my Kung Fu on him. However, I think what truly stopped him was my mother wanting to turn a profit by selling my virginity."

Annaliese spoke quickly, following their changing mood and conversation, "That's why I started back doing Kung Fu, to protect myself, especially from any more rapists. It's come in handy a few times already."

April said, "I can't believe how similar our lives have been."

Annaliese cut off her friends words by saying, "Yes, but you escaped. I did not. I became a victim. I still feel like one.

"All three of us faced similar situations, and we all reacted differently. Claire took her own life, I became a victim, but you April, you stood your ground and escaped unmolested."

In that instant their lightening mood was dashed. Annaliese's tears welled once more, and April wondered if her friend hated her for getting away, when she did not. April was about to say more,

Chapter 11

but Annaliese came into her arms and they held each other in comfortable and knowing silence.

Eventually the girls slept, but it was not good sleep, just the essential. April thought about getting ready for class, but knew she could not leave her best friend alone. Annaliese was vulnerable, not always focused, and mentioned getting a fix a couple of times. Like April, she hated drugs, but when things became too much for her, Annaliese felt obsessed with the need, the release.

April had to get them out of there. They walked out of the building well after midday, noticing the cops were making enquiries further up the street. Again, their trail was circuitous until April was sure no one was following them.

Chapter 12 – Recuperation

The girls arrived at the small town mid-afternoon, and Rosa smothered them immediately. She did not ask why they were there, but sent them to bathe and change, telling them she would prepare a special celebration dinner later.

After April showered, she found Annaliese helping in the kitchen, learning the ropes, the cuisine, and the language, just as she had done more than one year before. Rosa left Annaliese with many instructions, and came through to the adjoining living room with a brace of ice-cold San Miguel.

Rosa sat next to April on the sofa, looked at her, and said, "I know something has happened to the pair of you."

April's eyes flicked toward the kitchen and said, "It turned out all right in the end, but we both could have been raped by the hoods. But for our Kung Fu, she would have been. She has a past, I only just found out. She doesn't need lectures, she needs acceptance and support, and more than I alone can offer."

"Thank you for sharing, Chiquita, I know just what to do. Times of greatest adversity, also offer us unique chances to change our lives, if we could but see them at the time—but then, you know that already."

Rosa raised her voice. "Annaliese, turn the heat off. Come and drink this beer. Now!"

Rosa probed and questioned, as the girls both tried to evade her inquisition. Rosa should have been a detective. Eventually she pried from them the full story about the attempted rape a few nights before. April was not sure Rosa entirely believed them when they said they had fought the hoods off with Kung Fu, but she seemed to accept the story, at least for the time being.

Once they had admitted what happened, Rosa held them both, before saying, "You poor things, this is so unjust, but I admire and respect the pair of you. Now, I have to get dinner ready. Other people are depending on me."

Rosa sent Annaliese back to the kitchen with a load of orders, and sat closer beside April. She placed a hand on the girl's arm and looked her straight in the eye. "You did well to bring her here. I cannot believe it. Poor girl. We have talked and will talk again over the next few days. You are welcome to stay, but you know my magic works better one-on-one. Come back on Friday, Chiquita, and know all will be well."

Rosa stood and left, issuing more instructions as she entered the kitchen. She was forcing Annaliese to become a part of the here and now, and April knew she was right. April watched Annaliese, and could tell she was now working and learning. Her whole attitude was different from a few hours before.

April realized that wallowing in hurt and self-pity, had been replaced by the activity. Annaliese's life once more had worth, and others were depending upon her. April wondered at Rosa, and knew she was exceedingly clever when it came down to human animals—for an overly proud, ego-soaked animal is all that *homo sapiens* are.

Around 10 p.m., April wandered into the store and caught a guy trying to steal some cheap tequila. She marched him out and stayed until after midnight helping Marisol. Pepe had his one weekly night out with the boys, and Rosa was cooking out back.

The migrant farm help had mainly left, except for a few preparing for next planting. A small mine had reopened a few miles away, and this was the nearest town. This gave the girls a small rush ten minutes after twelve, and they closed at half past midnight.

They had already, practically cashed-up. Once the money was secure in the safe, they lowered the shutters and could relax.

The supper was fantastic, and Annaliese was proud of her efforts. Later, they shared April's single bed. Again Annaliese's tears, followed by nightmares, accompanied her friend's sleep. April realized her friend needed Rosa's focus on the present, and possible future's, not her reminders of the past.

§

April left midmorning, but skipped class and battered the Kung Fu wooden dummy for hours. Gary came to her a couple of times and improved her technique. The last time he asked, "April, why do you spend so much time working on this wooden dummy. You know there are more important skills you should be developing for your next belt."

April stopped and tried to answer, but wasn't sure what to say until she thought about it. Eventually she said, "*Sifu*, I like this repetitive series of movements. They flow naturally, and give me a space to let my mind wander, and bring me a sense of calm."

"I thought so. You are hurting inside, what happened to you?"

April shook her head, but added for her own clarity, as much as for Gary's understanding, "I have discovered the physical release of activity helps put my mind in order. I hope that doesn't sound strange, but it helps me a lot."

Gary seemed to accept that this was a release from emotional troubles. He did not press for information, like April had expected him to. Instead, he said, "Emotional healing is better addressed using The Way of the *Tao*, and learning to balance your *chi*. You are aware that hand to hand combat is only one of the five disciplines of Kung Fu?"

April said, "Yes *Sifu*, Kung Fu originated over five thousand years ago, and was initially the art of healing. Chinese medicine developed from this."

Gary was pleased, and added, "That is correct April, but Kung Fu also developed to heal the mind, and the soul. By learning a discipline like *Qi Gong*, which has nine central elements, you will become master of yourself, and your emotions, your body even. *Tai Chi* is a modern presentation of one of these nine forms."

April immediately put Annaliese's name down with her own for *Qi Gong* instruction. Gary told her that if enough people signed up, then an associate of his would run a course on campus.

April was back early the next morning, and Gary let her hit the stupid wood for a while before coming over and offering to teach her a new move. It was most difficult and April thought it would take months to master. However, Gary had given her a new challenge, and in between, somehow, she had moved on.

§

Friday night April slipped back to the apartment and showered in a hurry, intending to change quickly and catch the last bus back to Rosa's.

The knock at the door came as she was about finished. April told whomever, "Fuck off."

The reply was instant and forceful, "This is the police. Open up."

Chapter 12

She opened on the door chain and saw the uniform, before she focused on the badge. "Officer Dickerson, Ma'am. I need to ask you a few routine questions. May I come in?"

April spluttered apologies and opened the door properly, grousing that all kinds of creeps and weirdo's regularly knocked on her door late at night. He did not realize that April included him. With her secret joke safe, she felt confident, like an actress in a scene from a college play.

He checked her ID and other papers, verifying who she was on his radio. He proceeded to ask some questions, and enquired about the girl that shared the room. April said, "I live alone."

The room was in her name only, and she showed him the contract, but added, "Oh, my girlfriend stays over regularly for, you know." She waggled her eyebrows suggestively.

The cop stood motionless, and gave April a strange look as he absorbed the new information. April took the lead and began asking him what this was all about. "Just routine enquiries, Ma'am. There was a serious shooting a few nights ago near here. I don't suppose you heard anything, know anything about it?"

April played the fool, overdosing him with where and why questions, before becoming shocked, scared at his answers. She clung to him for safety, asking and hoping the Police would protect them all. He took it pretty well, and didn't ask about Annaliese again. April reckoned she was already two, or three steps ahead of him, and she thought he was more interested in escape. That suited her just perfectly.

The Officer turned to leave, informing April it was against his professional code to comfort a female, but offered her a number for counseling. Ye Gad's! April thought he was gone, but he spotted the wine and asked her if she had bought the bottles. Horrified, April replied that some guy who was keen on her had left them, and she confided in him, "I think he is plotting to try and get me drunk one night…"

April left the insinuation of her potential male lover hanging in the air, and the cop chuckled, letting it be. She thought he was done, but he sidestepped her. "Young lady, I need to take a look around, is that OK?"

April said, "Knock yourself out." She ignored him and pretended to do her own stuff. They did not have a TV, so she put on some music. She chose jazz, Trad and Cassandra Wilson. Cass knew all about this shit their young lives were being subjected to, and how.

Later, the cop turned in the doorway all fatherly-like, and stated to no one in particular, "Keep it in the refrigerator. Red wine should be slightly chilled, and Italian is best. Know it works well with cheese."

He tipped his cap to April and left. She watched him strut down the hallway, knowing never to trust a cop. She also knew not to judge all cops by the worst of them, since he was actually quite nice—in a cop sort of way.

April's last bus was gone already, and her hair within the head-towel was dry. She threw the turban away and shook her black locks, at last feeling free once more. She did not like the fact the police had been in the apartment, and wondered if they should consider moving. Through the shutters, she watched Officer Dickerson walk out to a regular police vehicle and drive off immediately. Game over.

April looked at both bottles, and opened the red from California, putting the Chilean one in the refrigerator. She would try this chilled, one time. Later that evening, she discovered that just sometimes, police officers tell the truth.

April thought about nuking some food, but nothing took her fancy. Besides, they did not have much of anything. She came back with an ashtray instead and smoked a cigarette. For the first time it felt good. She was calmer and felt more in control as the nicotine hit. She watched the smoke and knew some was blue, but what she exhaled was ghostly gray/brown; keeping the blue inside felt so right to her.

§

April worked out early Saturday morning, punching and kicking the wooden dummy into submission. She worked on form and later concentrated on the new move, knowing it wasn't right, but close.

Gary watched her for a while, but did not interrupt. She tried again, slightly off balance as she tried to flip backward by jumping forward. In that moment, April knew she could have kicked limbs off the wooden dummy with each of her feet, independently, as she

Chapter 12

curled over backwards, passing the horizontal. She had made the move. Yes! Her hand pumped back and up in victory.

It was awesome and extremely technical. Gary congratulated her, and left as soon as he saw she had been successful. Now her body instinctively knew how to do what had seemed impossible—a standing backwards somersault, where her body actually moved forward through the air. April knew in that moment she had to be with Annaliese to celebrate.

Chapter 13 – Missing

April showed up at Rosa's a day later than planned, refreshed, and ready to see her truest friends and family, barring her father of course. Annaliese was running the store single-handed and needed help. She was new and the patrons knew it. April barred the door and stopped everyone from leaving before they put back what they had stolen. She knew the regular faces, and identified two new thieves.

One cocky, short-assed migrant tried to get it on with her. "Tia Buena. ¿You wanna search me for it, Conchita? " He ended up on his back before he knew what hit him. He said it in the wrong way, and April had understood the sexual jibe.

April had drawn back her fist for a heart punch when Annaliese screamed "No!" April was mighty pissed. She searched the guy, and found he had stolen twice as much as he had bought. She took his wallet and only as much cash as he owed the store, before dragging him out into the dust outside the door.

Annaliese and April kissed as soon as they could, but the store was busy and they abandoned trying to catch up, leaving it until later. When there was a lull, Annaliese said, "Rosa's husband and children are crossing the border today."

April had not known she had either. Annaliese continued to fill her in, "Rosa left a short time ago knowing you would be back soon. She has gone to meet them in Tepin's car and left us the pickup truck. Marisol and Pepe went with her—they are a close family. She said they would be back tomorrow morning."

Customers kept coming so they stayed open. Things got quiet around 2:30 the next morning, and they closed for a few hours. The miners began banging the shutter at 5:30 a.m., looking for food before their 6 a.m. shift at the mine. They were working eighteen-hour days and were paid a pittance, but it was gold to them and their families back in Mexico.

April realized the market was staying open 24/7. As the only Mexican cook, she started preparing tacos, tortillas, and burritos for the 12 midnight and 6 a.m. shifts. This soon became the midday and 6 p.m. shifts also, four eighteen hour work rotations per day.

Chapter 13

The girls did the math, and offered the best they could. Annaliese learned fast, and they shared the work so they could each sleep sometimes, but never together.

Rosa was a day overdue, and they were both desperately worried about her. They knew something bad must have happened to her. Neither girl was particularly religious, but April did spend a moment at the small shrine and sent a wish for Rosa's God to look out for her. She did not think an omnipotent being would have the slightest interest in their small lives, but she felt comforted afterwards.

§

Teves popped in one afternoon, and asked where Rosa was. April remembered how adults had always answered her questions when she was a child. She told him only what he needed to know, "Rosa went to see her husband and children, and Pepe and Marisol went with her."

Teves nodded distractedly, got a coffee from the machine, and bought a few snacks. When he came back to the cash register he said, "She hasn't seen her family for a long time. I am sure they will have a great time in Mexico. How long will she be gone, April?"

The girls had no idea if she was even alive, but if Teves thought they were all in Mexico, that suited them just fine. Annaliese answered, "We don't know Officer. She left in such a hurry and asked us to mind the store until she got back."

Teves thought for a moment, and became concerned, "I know her father is old and not in the best of health. I hope nothing has happened to him. He is a lovely man, her mother also, although I only met them once. That was in this town, one Christmas many years back. We had a great evening, all of the locals celebrated in the town square."

He smiled knowingly and said as an aside, "We Mexicans know how to party you know. Last Christmas…"

§

A few days later, the workers' bus, an opened backed truck, started making a regular stop to pick up workers from the store's front yard. April had gotten a few tables reconditioned by a local carpenter, so people could eat outside in comfort and perhaps be encouraged to buy a little more in store, and they did.

Their impromptu restaurant flourished and April became aware many of the workers needed accommodation. They often curled up on the ground outside and slept. She spent some money for mattresses and set them against the wall of the yard at the side of the store. She charged them but a few dollars, just to cover her outlay. The next evening it rained a deluge. April paid the carpenter to put the mattresses on top of solid frames. They tented roofs and sides with wooden poles and plastic tarps. It was crude, but it was better than sleeping in the dust.

They had been worried frantic about Rosa the whole week. April's Smartphone had internet browser and email, but her pay as you go sim did not. She doubted the town could muster more than one typewriter, never mind a computer with internet connection.

The next morning they saw Marisol staggering towards the front steps, her hair a tangled mess, her body badly wounded from both beating and gunshots. She was barely alive except for her courage. One foot was dragging a bloody trail, and with it marked her gritty determination to get a message back.

The girls closed and shuttered the store immediately, scrawling a sign to say they would be open again later. The official clinic was a waste of space and closed as usual. April got the address of a proper doctor from the information wall, and loaded Marisol into Rosa's pickup. The doctor had a Mexican name and April spoke to him in local Spanish. Minutes later she gave him some of the money they had taken from the hoods. The attempted rape had its unforeseen rewards.

The doctor took them to one side and shook his head sadly, "It is touch and go whether your friend will live."

"Is there anything we can do to help her?" April asked.

"Hold her hand. Let her know you are here, that she is now safe." He advised.

April wiped Marisol's brow with a moist cloth, remembering how her own father had done the same for her a few years before.

Annaliese held Marisol's hand. They talked quietly, but confidently, and April saw the girl slightly squeeze her friend's hand. Marisol had been unable to say a word, and the girls'

concern heightened with each passing moment. The sedative was
starting to take effect, so they headed back and reopened the store.

They were greatly distressed about Rosa, and had not been
able to learn anything from Marisol. Given her condition they
feared the worst, that Rosa had been killed. Nevertheless, life went
on, and in times of deepest anguish, being active helped a lot. It
took their minds off-of imagining what may have happened.

Annaliese checked on Marisol midmorning, and April went
after the early evening rush. Marisol's condition was still critical,
the doctor stating it was fifty-fifty whether she would last the
night. April was deeply worried, but there was nothing she could
do except spend time with her newest friend. April spoke words of
encouragement, and nonsense, as she wiped Marisol's brow once
more.

The following morning the doctor had some hopeful news,
"She has stabilized overnight and may pull through."

"What about the bullets?" April asked. "When can you take
those out?"

"I don't have a nurse and we can't move her to a real hospital."

"If you need a nurse, I can do that for her," April replied
without consideration. She looked at her friend lying on the bed
and tried not to think of the blood. The doctor showed her where to
scrub up and she drenched her hands in alcohol.

As April prepared, she tried to regret her hastily spoken offer
of assistance, but she could not. Marisol was a friend in greatest
need. Instead, she looked at herself in the mirror and said, "Be
strong girl, this will all be over soon, and it will help save
Marisol's life."

"We'll start with the easy one first. Thank God she's still
unconscious," the doctor said, opening his roll of tools. The bullet
in her leg came out easily and he sewed the wound up. The one in
her abdomen was the problem.

Marisol was cut open and the bullet located in her liver. April
had to hold, swab, and pass tools as requested. It was gross, but her
friend was most important. Eventually, the doctor teased the lead
out from its hiding place, near a major artery. He removed the
bullet, sewed up, and crossed himself.

By the next day Marisol was conscious, and the following
evening she could speak to April, if only briefly. Her words were

stuttered but she croaked, "Rosa, Pepe OK. Caught crossing, border patrol."

The effort was too much for her, and April was ushered away immediately, as Marisol was sedated once more. However, those few words lifted her spirit tremendously. She ran back to the store to break the good news to Annaliese.

Marisol stayed two more days before the doctor delivered her to the store. April paid him for his extra work and care, which left a large dent in their savings, but it was money well spent.

Later the next evening Marisol was able to tell the story. "We went down to the crossing point, the same place where Pepe and I had crossed over into the States. It was great to see my uncle and cousins again, understand, we are a close community as well as greater family.

"Our joy of reunion was cut short as bullets rang out from the darkness. A bounty hunter, gone vigilante searching for illegals, confronted us. There was no chance to run, as the man was an extremely good shot, even in the darkness. I was forced to tie the others up, before he did likewise with me. He called on his headset for his sidekick to bring the wagon, before he proceeded to retie everyone else.

"The pair of them searched us, and they discovered Rosa's legitimate ID. He spat at her and told her it was fake, throwing it away into the brush. I know exactly where it landed. They stole all of our money and jewelry, including my engagement ring."

Marisol broke down and wept. Not a deluge, but Annaliese and April both knew it was not just the robbery, but represented the rape of something she held most dear. The girls comforted Marisol accordingly, and once she felt stronger, she continued.

"We stopped for gas as we neared El Cajon. All doors were automatically unlocked, and I made a run for it when everyone was preoccupied. I almost made it to safety, but the bounty hunter shot me in the leg. I fell and tumbled down a ravine, banging the back of my neck on a sharp rock as I came to rest. I was immediately unconscious.

"I can only guess he saw the pool of blood running down the rock and presumed that my head was crushed. It was actually a cactus cut to my ear, so I guess he did not come all the way down to check on me. He must have shot me again as I lay prone. When I recover, I am so going to kill that bastard.

Chapter 13

"It was dark when I woke. I was in agony but could not trust anyone. I holed up for a few days to get my strength back and roughly treat my wounds. I got on a freight train to San Diego, before I borrowed a vehicle. That got me close to the turn off for the road to here, before it ran out of gas. I had to hide my trail and wanted the owner to get his vehicle back. I staggered and crawled the rest of the way back, but remember little of it through the pain and tears. Thank you for saving my life."

She wilted and they carried her through to her room. She gradually improved, but it was a slow recovery. By the next week, she was able to cook sometimes, and help on the till for a few hours. With Marisol's added hands, Annaliese and April managed to sleep a bit longer, but Rosa's store was now the sum total of their existence.

Chapter 14 – Keeping Up Appearances

Teves continued to drop by a couple of times each week, and usually enquired after Rosa. The girls had nothing to tell him, and he accepted that. Marisol went inside whenever one of them saw his cruiser, so their cover story remained safe.

Teves was becoming more interested in the mine, and always asked them what the mineworkers talked about. April said, "There isn't much to tell. They may be illegals, but you don't seem to be interested in that. I know that they work long hours, and do hard work, and don't like to sleep there. I feel sorry for them, and we try to offer what they want at prices they can afford."

Teves nodded, but added, "I don't know what it is, but there's something wrong about this whole thing. I've been to the mine, but there are areas I'm not allowed to go into without a warrant. They tell me it is to do with insurance, health and safety, that sort of thing, but I think there is something more."

He removed his cap and scratched his head, looking into the distance for a moment. He looked back at them, fixing both April and Annaliese in the eye, before saying, "Girls, we are friends, right? I am not interested in the workers themselves, OK. I am interested in anything, let us say, unusual, that they should let slip, say about the mine itself, or the management. I am not asking you to snitch on anyone, just tell me if they say anything odd. Thank you. And thank you for looking out for them. Rosa will be so proud of you when she returns. You got any idea when that will be?"

April said, "No, Sir, she has not been in touch with us yet."

Teves accepted her words at face value, but added in a fatherly manner, "I hope you girls are not jeopardizing your studies because of this?"

April smiled reassuringly and answered directly, "Of course not, we both go up to San Diego a couple of times each week."

Teves grunted approvingly, and went off to visit the mine. The girls talked about their lives, and they knew they each owed a debt to Rosa. All the same, Teves had a valid point. They had to keep up with studies, and ROTC, or they would drop a year and certainly lose their scholarships. This was becoming serious.

April told Annaliese to return to SDSU now that Marisol was getting better, but her friend had other plans. She went back for one day, intending to cancel her course, but was told she could get the tutorials and coursework online. ROTC were supportive, although she told them little of worth. Annaliese spent an hour on the range with one of the sergeants, and buffed her credentials so they were not worried about her. She returned with all of her worldly possessions and some college stuff.

April went back the next day and did likewise. The main problem was with The School of Theatre, Television, and Film. She was studying theater as a minor, so she had to be there every Wednesday afternoon for "practical theatrical arts," meaning they were rehearsing to perform a play as the core of the assessment, when the rest of the campus was doing sports.

Later April saw the student advisor, who offered to be available online. He seemed rather shocked when she informed him she didn't have a TV, never mind a computer. He gave her an odd look, and his business card with email address. April knew at once she needed to get connected. She went to a discount store to buy a new Smartphone sim with full connectivity, and came out with a great deal on a tablet computer as well.

She wandered downtown hoping her father might be around, but of course, he wasn't. She looked in store windows at things she could not afford, and wasn't sure she wanted either. She was soaking up the image of appearing normal once more. The people around her in their bustling gallop of life made this appear even more real.

April stopped to buy a fajita at a street stall, and it was awful. An American copy of the real thing she now loved. She threw it away and was slowly headed towards the apartment, when she noticed cops out for some stop and frisk fun. They were picking on students, blacks, and Mexicans as usual. April had nothing to hide, but she did not want to play their games.

April veered into a mall and came out the other side, where more cops were also in for some searching fun. She heard the sound of someone following her and crossed the road instinctively. April wasn't quite sure where she was, so stopped at a bus stop to look at the map. The bus to Rosa's pulled up almost at once, and she got the hell out of there.

Later she mused, "Me, Paranoid? I do think so. However, I am becoming extremely conscious of who is looking out for me, and why."

Back at Rosa's store, April doubted either of her purchases would connect, but they both did immediately. Someone nearby had an unsecured Wi-Fi connection, and large bandwidth. Now that they had news from Marisol, April could only presume that Rosa had either been deported, or was in a U.S. prison. Since she at last had connection, she searched the internet, and discovered the Sheriff's Department of San Diego also ran the prison service. She looked up their website, and found they had a prisoner tracking system. All she had to do was enter the person's full name. April typed in "Rosario Ascension de Açuna," and got a hit straight away.

She was disappointed she could not get any further information, but at least Rosa was still alive. This was great news. She told both Annaliese and Marisol at once. From this they presumed that Pepe and the others must have been deported back to Mexico.

April spent all of the next Wednesday on campus, the morning on library research for her mounting pile of projects. She saw the student advisor briefly, and attended the group production.

She also bought a small laptop for Annaliese, as she preferred pressing physical keys for some strange reason. April added a couple of 16 GB USB drives, and headed back to clear the apartment. Immediately, she was taken aside and asked to pay the back-rent. Stunned, she was lost until she realized that the month had moved on, and money was due.

She apologized, but said that she had moved out and was only back to collect her last remaining stuff. The duty scum ball pressured her for a full month's rent all the same, which she knew would end up in his back pocket. April slapped a hundred dollar bill down on the counter, but kept her hand upon it, calling him out, "This is yours so long as you forget me."

The slime-ball was unmoved, that was, until April started to take it back. With that his mood changed instantly and he ingratiatingly took the bribe. April had twenty minutes or the deal was off. April headed for their room, but he called her back, "This package arrived for you, and I need to get rid of it."

The postmark was interstate and over two weeks old. Pond scum. He looked at his watch and stated, "Nineteen minutes, fifteen seconds, and counting..."

Chapter 14

April knew something was wrong as soon as she turned the key in the lock; it clinked if it has been locked from the inside. It clinked for sure. She slowly opened the door, stopping just before the hinges would creak, and gingerly sidestepped inside with her gun already drawn, and safety off. There was a large bulk inside the bed.

She knew it was a man because of the large pair of jeans strewn on the floor, and man's shirt nearby. "Had the jerk at the desk already rented the place with all their stuff still in it, or was this another rapist?" she wondered.

Such was her life and view of this fucked-up world. The guy was snoring and oblivious to her presence. She dropped her purchases, and ever so quietly, closed and relocked the door. She never once took her eyes off the home invader. She ventured nearer, but his face was buried deep within the covers.

April stared at the covered body for some moments, trying to determine if it was her father, but it was not. Whoever it was, was smaller.

She was distracted by a sound near the foot of the bed, and the movement of a dark and bulky monster, as it rose from deep sleep on stiff legs, and stretched.

April threw the gun down and rushed to smother him, his awakening face like that of a puppy. Satan shook his head and greeted April's hug like the true friend she was. She was soon on her back, her face being licked to death.

Satan was excited and wanted to play. April needed to distract his *lurve*, and get all of them the hell out of there. The clock was ticking. She went to the refrigerator, and threw him the remains of a large cake she knew they would never eat. It was chocolate, his favorite.

John was hardly rousing in the bed, so April shook him awake and said, "We have to leave in ten, my rental is up, and I am on borrowed time."

She turned and walked away, while asking over her shoulder if he wanted instant or beer. John did not reply, so she got the last two beers out of the refrigerator and flicked both open. April cleared most of the little remaining stuff as he came awake and dressed. She sat down and lit a cigarette. John came over to join her, and she indicated the open packet and for him to help himself.

He lit one and took a deep draw, commenting, "Same brand as your father. He's still stuck up in Seattle, but should be cleared soon. They are dragging things out to make his life as awkward as can be, a sort of unofficial punishment if you like.

"They took his regular cell phone, but found nothing on it. However, it has not been returned to him, so he sent you a burner cell. When you did not answer, he asked me to come down and check if you were all right."

April said, "Yeah. A lot of stuff has happened, but both Annaliese and I are fine. I just picked up the burner cell Dad sent through weeks ago, I guess it's out of date by now."

April's eyes fixed on the clock, as she absentmindedly rolled the end of her cigarette in the ashtray, putting it out in the process, and finishing her beer. She looked at John with urgency, and said, "I have to be out of here in five. You clear the trash, take what's by the door, and I'll get the rest of the stuff. Deal." It was not a question.

John left, taking her pile by the door. April was done, but at the last moment remembered the fridge and freezer. She piled everything into a carrier and left. In the foyer, the guy was upset. She was one minute early. April handed over the keys thinking their deal complete. The scum-ball took them and went to check the room. April followed at his bidding.

The low-life tried to bill her for cleaning, but April told him to get lost. He locked the door and dropped his trousers, telling her to suck. April dropped to her knees like a good little girl, and punched his man parts as hard as she could. The ape cursed her as he doubled over, "I'll tell the cops on you."

She stopped, and returned to alter his awareness. April drew her gun and placed it at his temple; she pulled the trigger. The hammer fell. 'Click'. "Next time there will be a bullet in that chamber, Punk."

April left at once and never looked back. She jumped into the passenger seat as John hit the gas pedal. He wanted to take April home to Rosa's, but she stated for security reasons, that she needed to arrive, as normal, by bus. His pickup truck would stand out a mile.

John understood at once, since in most small towns, everybody knew everyone else's business. April was aware John knew roughly, where she now lived, because they had talked at some

Chapter 14

depth. If she did not have a father, she would have chosen John. April told him that her new Mother was missing, but glossed over the details.

John dropped her at an interchange off the highway. It was handy for his return journey. April had traveled the local road many times before, and knew exactly where the bus to the Rosa's would stop.

She opened the door, but stopped and slid around to kiss him full on the lips. It was not a sexual kiss, but it could have been, had he responded. As it was, he did not, so, her known world and womanhood remained in place. April kissed Satan also, not wanting him to be jealous. She slammed the door shut behind her, and was gone.

She tried not to, but she just had to look back. April waved at the disappearing truck, and wondered what might have been.

Chapter 15 – The Best Christmas Present Ever

People can be protected from everything but themselves. Truly loving them means believing in them, picking up the pieces and sticking them back together again.

April was sure she did this for Annaliese, but her friend remained adamant she did it for April. People may have thought they were both fucked, but they were stuck back together; two young girls, one mission: survival.

Meanwhile, Marisol came back to life, but there was always some essential spark missing from the fun-loving girl they had known before. Ghosts and memories haunted her. The year was moving towards Christmas, and everybody but they, were looking forward to the Festival.

In San Diego, people embraced shopping and the face of the holiday, while forgetting to mention one man in any meaningful thought of passing. Jesus. April found that dreadfully depressing.

Back in their small town, the long Christmas celebrations began on December 12 with the feast of La Guadalupana. The nine days of Las Posadas began on the sixteenth, which commemorated the Biblical New Testament story of Joseph and Mary's search for shelter in Bethlehem. It consisted of candlelight processions, as well as stops at various nativity scenes that had been erected around the town.

During this time, Deputy Teves wandered into the store, but did not say 'Hello' as normal. He went straight to the coffee machine and made himself a drink. He hollered into the living area, "Marisol, you can come out now."

The girl sheepishly crept out from hiding, eyes downcast, not looking at him. Teves took a drink of his coffee and put it down, leaning on the counter to look at each of the girls in turn. There was a teasing smile on his face, but it was clear by his eyes he was mighty pissed.

He straightened and said, "Girls. I had a most interesting chat with my opposite number down in Chula Vista today. You'll never guess what he told me, or perhaps you can?"

April tried to speak, but he cut her off instantly, "I thought we were good friends. I do not like being messed about. You know the saying, 'the truth will out'. Well today, your truth was outed, and I am not impressed with any of you."

Chapter 15

This time they all tried to speak, but Teves shouted over their meek protestations, "If you had told me what was going on, I could have done something about it. As it stands, by the time I can act, it will be Christmas, and everyone in authority will be either on vacation, or have no time to spare for what is, essentially, a petty crime. I could probably have got that crime quashed, had I known before the hearing."

Teves stopped to stare at his victims menacingly. April grabbed the moment as he drank his coffee, and said, "Deputy Teves, Undersheriff, we never intended to trick you, we just didn't know what had happened to Rosa, until Marisol returned. Even then, it was only a couple of days ago I managed to find out where she was. We were worried sick about her if you must know."

His crocodile smile returned, calling them out, "Then why didn't you tell me?"

Teves finished his coffee as they all tried to speak at the same time. He held up his hand and said, "Silence! Because of my good nature, and my deep respect for Rosa, I will write this off as being a simple misunderstanding. Perhaps it was originally, on my part. Trust me in the future. Do you understand? Good day, Ladies!"

The girls were shocked. They never knew there was another side to Teves, one that could kill a person with a glance. His words stung, and they knew they had got it wrong. But what else could they have done?

The girls were kept busy. They both had final examinations, and module submissions due before the winter recess. College was the best place to study, and one of their ROTC classmates usually enjoyed the company of one of them each weekday evening.

April had to leave the store for one foreshortened week and attend rehearsals. Hers was a small part of no worth, but she had studied the whole play and knew it by heart. One of the main supporting actresses wouldn't be available for the opening night. Apparently she got locked-up by the cops who caught her in the act of snorting crack. With one rehearsal to go before the curtain rose, April was selected for the part, knowing the words better than her peers. She swore inwardly, "Having an eidetic memory can become a curse sometimes."

The speaking part was not a problem, she had a perfect memory, but the acting took its toll. She scraped through the first night, and improved much on the second day, a matinee performance. By the final performance, April had the part in her own character and it was becoming easy and fun.

The celebrations afterwards were crap. Movie and theater creeps hit on her too often. She instantly said "NO!" to whatever they offered, although she did keep the business cards she was handed by a couple of the more sincere professionals among the throng. Unlike everybody else hoping to head for the bright lights of LA, by the end of the night, April was grateful to return to the normality of Rosa's store. She already knew what LA was all about.

§

Despite the offer of extra money to work through the festive season, mineworkers were drifting away to spend Christmas with their families in Mexico. First, the mine canceled the nightshift, but they were soon forced to close digging operations until after January 6. At Rosa's store, the girls were able to close for the first time in months, and it was a great relief to all of them.

By the late afternoon, two days before Christmas Eve, no one was out on the streets. The place felt like a ghost town. The population was one third of its normal size, and the remaining residents were preparing to celebrate the festive season with close family and the Church. Most were passionate Roman Catholics, a form of worshipping Jesus and God that Annaliese and April knew little about.

The following day, one person came during the normal morning rush, and they knew that staying open was a waste of time. April closed the shutters and hung a sign outside, with their landline number for service. Nobody called for ages. They opened for a couple of people, but chilled and enjoyed what amounted to their first day off in centuries. Marisol went to church that evening, and the girls relaxed in front of the recently bought TV. It showed crowds thronging to shops to pay homage to the Western, commercialized version of Christmas. They laughed and ridiculed their own heritage for being so self-absorbed.

The time was after nine when April started to worry, but Annaliese said, "Marisol is probably just enjoying socializing for a change. Let her be April."

Chapter 15

Twenty minutes later, the phone rang and it was a man on the line. April said she would open the store, but the man laughed and said he wanted to give them a Christmas present.

Although he sounded harmless and familiar, the girls took no chances, Annaliese opening the store door shutter, while April hung back with her gun primed and ready to fire.

The man turned out to be Tepin. He stepped aside and Annaliese let out a whoop of joy, rushing to hug the person before her. April stood her ground until Annaliese tore herself away and dragged Rosa back into her domain. April was soon clinging to Rosa, asking a torrent of questions, until her tears came unbidden, and she held her spiritual mother far too tightly.

Marisol brought Tepin through to share the reunion. Apparently, they had met Marisol in church and spent time to catch up briefly after the service. They all helped unload Tepin's pickup. The cargo was mainly quality Mexican red wine, plus an assortment of better Mexican beers, Brandy, and Tequila. The rest of the bulk consisted of exotic fruit and vegetables they had bought in Chula Vista. There was also a lot of flour and sugar, plus an assortment of the weirdest herbs and spices April had ever laid eyes upon. She doubted they would sell any of it before next New Year, but Rosa knew her business and it was not for her to comment.

Once settled, Rosa got out an old box and created a nativity scene from the contents. Later they all prayed joyfully, while April and Annaliese cooked. Once they had eaten, they finally got to hear what had happened to Rosa.

"My husband and the children got through at our secret crossing place, and it was wonderful to be with them again. I guess we were so happy and distracted we did not take the usual precautions. We were fired upon by a bounty hunter and taken. I thought Pepe was still free, but the guy's accomplice already had him.

"When we stopped for gas, Marisol made a run for it and almost made it, but I saw her fall and knew she must be dead. My senses left me. In the beginning, I told the authorities I was an American citizen, but with my driver's license thrown away by our captor, I could not prove it. We were in lockup for several days. Finally, we got a lawyer and he advised me to change my story. He told me the kids would be sent back to our village in Mexico, but the fate of the rest of us was uncertain.

"Our crossing place had been highlighted, and included in regular deputy patrols. One cop who knew of our case found my ID, and that is when my life changed. After a short hearing, my husband was sent back at once to our village with our children, still technically minors, although they would be as old as you two really are." Rosa looked up and nodded at Annaliese and April.

Within the confirmation, she continued, "Pepe was treated harshly and sent to the remotest part of Mexico under the new Consequence Delivery System. All their details were also lodged with Mexican, and obviously U.S. authorities.

"To me it is an injustice, because the local economy hereabouts would collapse without us. Can you imagine Americans working twelve and eighteen-hour days, every single day, at that reopened mine, for a pittance. They would not do it. Same with the fruit picking at harvest time, they need the Cuadrillas, or the price of everything would double, even triple overnight."

Everyone talked about the injustice briefly, before homing in on the implicit double standard. April changed the subject, and said, "Rosa, I wholeheartedly agree, but let's pick this up another time. What happened to you?"

Rosa took a deep breath, which was unusual for her, and spoke again, "I was accepted as being an American citizen, and I thought they would free me. Instead, I was charged with assisting illegal immigrants to enter the country and was fined harshly. I chose not pay the fine, so was sent to prison. I got out only yesterday, and let me tell you, I am never going back."

Rosa cried as she confessed small details of her incarceration, and everyone took turns to hold her. As she stilled, she revealed, "Tepin is one of the few people I know and trust, who is also a legitimate U.S. citizen. The only one I trust implicitly. He was waiting for me when I got out, and brought me home."

April looked up at the old man with newfound reverence, and promised to never judge another without knowing them properly again. Tepin smiled deprecatingly, his personal honor plain to see.

Everybody celebrated that night, and they all got merrily drunk in the happiest of times. The phone began ringing just before 6.30 a.m. on Nochebuena, and minutes later, the store opened as normal. People were seeking ingredients, last minute cards, and

Chapter 15

little gifts. Everyone stopped to welcome Rosa back. This was the only store in town, and stocked just about everything. The weird herbs, fruit, and vegetables were in great demand, as were the bottles of good Mexican red they now stocked.

Meanwhile, Rosa went over the books and was amazed at the increase in turnover. April told her about the new mining company, and that they were open twenty-four seven nowadays. Rosa inspected the beds they had arranged and complimented them on their business skills.

Rosa soon returned to the kitchen working with Tepin and Marisol, making what appeared to be a feast for the whole township. The girls had their last customer a little before 1 p.m., and stayed open a few minutes longer, before placing the 'CLOSED' sign back on the door and locking up.

They enjoyed lunch before two. It was the same mix of tamales (chicken and fruit versions) accompanied by atole, chili's, tacos, menudo, carne asada, enchiladas, chalupas, and beans as normal, but a lot more intricate. Most of it was sweeter also, and there were special breads on offer like buñuelos. Rosa also served Ponche Navideño, a special Mexican Christmas punch that was full of exotic fruits, nuts, and an awful lot of brandy. It was delicious and quite addictive.

In time, everyone was stuffed, and the siesta that followed was most welcome. Rosa roused everybody at 6 p.m. to get ready for church. Annaliese and April were both becoming keen pagans, so they tried to get out of it, but Rosa insisted they all go together.

April was stunned. Compared to the pretend posturing of the religion she had known from childhood, this was uplifting. The preacher talked about God, Jesus, and explained, if in Spanish, or sometimes Latin, the deeper meanings of Christmas. April wished she could state she was not moved, but she was.

As she walked outside afterwards, Annaliese said, "That was different. Have you noticed, there is no commercialism in this town?"

April replied, "Yes. Weird isn't it. They are actually celebrating Christmas, and the true meanings behind it. The only pressure we had was from the Town Manager, who came round personally collecting alms to give to the poor."

Annaliese was quick to respond, "Yes that's true, and Rosa of course who insisted we come here to church. They believe in God, and practice social caring and charity here. I bet no girl hereabouts has ever been raped either."

April responded, "I bet. D'you think that is because this small community is a lot closer to each other than our own. Perhaps their faith prevents them from doing anything seriously wrong. Shhh, Teves is coming over for a chat."

Once the girls were alone and outside, April looked around. The church was set centrally at one end of a small town square, a short walkway leading into it from the only road. Opposite was the lockup and part-time jail, and in between were about one hundred simple wooden tables with a large space in the middle. The square was lit-up, and food was being prepared to one side near the community health center, and opposite the Town Hall.

Rosa had been circulating, but rushed over when she saw them, "I have work for idle hands, come. We will party later. But first we make a lot of money. They will hold a piñata, a children's party now, although the main one will be tomorrow midday. Come."

Tepin drove the pickup, and the girls sat in the back. They were given instructions to open the store for one hour.

Hardly to their astonishment, there was a run on alcohol. Annaliese made countless trips to the storeroom to try and keep the shelves stocked, eventually dragging through a pallet truck full of wine boxes. Marisol and April worked the counter in tandem, she taking the money while April filled the carriers and packed. It was not difficult as most were buying boxes of Mexican red wine, which Rosa had put on special offer. It was actually cheaper to buy all twelve bottles individually, but the cases flew out the door.

Rosa soon returned, having donated a mountain of food to the celebration and rode shotgun over the store, keeping the hordes in line. By the time they got back to the square, celebrations were well under way. A band was playing a strange mixture of hymns and Latin carnival music, and those who had finished eating got up to sing and dance in the plaza.

There were a few short speeches just before eleven o'clock, followed by la Misa Del Gallo, 'the rooster's mass'. It was most unlike the previous sermon, and consisted mainly of carols, anecdotes, and a further collection of alms for the poor. Unlike the formal western version, people were urged to their feet, some dancing in celebration, and everybody sang.

Chapter 15

At five to midnight, the Priest gave a public blessing, and everyone stopped for a one-minute silent contemplation. At the stroke of midnight the church bells rang out, and then all hell broke loose. The band started up again and people thronged to the dance floor. Everybody drank, danced, and had a great time. There were few boys their own age, but Annaliese and April got good Latin dancing instruction from two of the esteemed community leaders. April was captured and became enthralled by Teves, who certainly knew how to dance and enjoy a party, as did his family.

He also knew how to drink. They sat down several times to catch their breath and take on a slug or two of beer with Tequila chasers. The atmosphere was carnival, but April took a quiet moment aside to apologize to Teves about the deception and Rosa's disappearance. It was like a confession, but one between a father and daughter.

Bridges were repaired, and trust between them grew once more. Talk naturally led on to the miners. Teves said, "It is strange there are only Caucasian bosses, and Mexican workers. There is nothing in between."

April told him what she knew, but it was little or nothing. However, their open sharing moved their relationship along—that was, until Teves heard the strains of the Tango, and dragged April protesting to her feet. She tried to escape, but Xochitl, Teves' wife, grabbed her free hand and led her towards her dancing doom.

What a blast! By the time the party broke up many hours later, April was on first name terms with Teves. She had to admit, Manny was OK in a social setting, and his family were gorgeous; his wife could Tango for Latin America!

Santa Claus did not call, but then, they already had the best Christmas present, ever.

The Mexican Christmas finished on January 6 with Día de los Santos Reyes, or Epiphany, when the Three Wise Men appeared to baby Jesus. April knew of it by its literary name, Twelfth Night. Once festivities were over, Rosa sent the girls back to college with instructions to excel.

Chapter 16 – Recurring Nightmares

Students, migrant workers, and misfits had taken all the vacant rooms before they got back to San Diego. The girls managed, for a week, switching between the library and theater underworld. April had the money to pay for a room, but there were none to be had.

On the final night, they were asleep under the stage, when the lights went on. They were groggy and disoriented, trying to come awake. A girl said to the leader, "Damon, there she is. I told you they would be in here."

"We owe you, Shirl."

Five jocks rushed them, pinning them down inside their sleeping bags. April recognized two of them from the Halloween Party, and Shirl, the girl who had spiked her drink.

The jock she had kicked under the chin sat astride her belly and said, "I have you this time bi-otch. Time for us to have a little fun, you're gonna get some man-meat, ready or not. Tie 'em and strip 'em lads, let's make 'em jock hoes."

Both girls were by then wide-awake, but trapped. April struggling to free herself, to find space to fight. Annaliese had frozen, her mind had shut down. They were rolled over onto their stomachs and held securely, as the zippers of their sleeping bags were lowered, and hands reached inwards for their wrists.

The girl encouraged the jocks, shouting, "That's it, get the bitch, break her. I'll video this."

Shirl bent to April's eye line and spat, "You gonna be a movie star Hon, and your friend. Yeah. Gotta website called Aztec Campus Hoes, and you two are the next hot stuff. You gonna make us a lot of money once you're trained and start turning tricks for us."

April spat in her eye, bit her hand, and managed to turn, freeing her right hand, but keeping it hidden, away from her attackers. With leverage, she head-butted the girl in the mouth, and twisted violently, throwing the man on top of her into a heap nearby.

Annaliese had finally come alive, but the jocks were already trying to tie her hands behind her back. She wriggled and turned, but she did not have the strength to free herself.

April leaped out of the bag and kicked the nearest person, the girl, under the ear, sending her flying into the jocks assaulting

Chapter 16

Annaliese. The two guys who had been trying to subdue her friend, rushed April. She dove and almost got free, but one held her ankle and she could not kick his grip free with her other foot. April's advantage was lost, too eager to assist Annaliese.

April cursed herself for being so stupid, before she switched tactics; she had been trying to pull away. The only way to attack was to move forward, towards her tormentors. Sliding her butt along, she bent her knees, and pushed up with her arms as hard as she could, throwing her weight forward to assist her stand, like the progression of a sit-up.

Before she was properly on her feet, her free leg swung and her heel hammered full-force into the wrist of the jock holding her ankle. He screamed out in pain. April freewheeled away as another jock football tackled her. His fingers raked her flesh as he fell badly in the space she had occupied a split-second before.

Another body crashed into her before she knew what was happening, and held her down. Other hands reached for her within the scrum, overpowered her, and her hands were tied tight behind her back. She was rolled over onto her back, and froze, the knife pointed at her face. Shirl laughed in her face as she moved the knife towards April's PJ's. The rip of fabric pulled on her chest before giving way; "We got her ready for you Damon."

April searched valiantly, but vainly for any means of escape. Damon stood over her, and slowly began to unbuckle his belt. He stopped and looked her in the eye, before his face morphed into that of a monster. "In a minute sweetheart, don't be impatient. You will have to wait for my lurve. First I owe you something from way back, bitch."

He kicked her jaw with full force. April was, and was not conscious, she floated in between. Her body was dead to the world. She knew her PJ's were being cut away, the jocks drinking beer from bottles as they laughed, egging each other on. They continued enthusing about what they were about to do to her, to them both.

April was soon naked, but her mind was coming back, her conscious clearing, but what could she do in such a vulnerable situation? She had remained still, plotting her next move. The mocking, jeering jocks laughed at her impending doom, "Time to become a jock hoe Hon, ain't nothing gonna save you now,"

Damon mouthed-off. "Spread her legs, I been looking forward to taking this bi-otch for a long time."

One of the intruders said, "No man, stop. I ain't in to this shit, this isn't fun, it's rape. I'm leaving."

Damon turned around "Is that so, Davy. I'm the team Captain, regardless of your big-shot pappy. I say who's on the team, and who isn't. You wanna tell your parents why you were dropped? Not good enough to be a jock? Huh."

As focus turned to the turncoat, April realized he was the only real man amongst them. Her peripheral vision saw Annaliese surreptitiously change her position. With a quick movement, Liese managed to bring her legs through her hands, and rested them on her stomach. April gave some lip, and getting more back, she had ensured the jocks full attention was on her.

Their tormentors distracted, Annaliese rose and kicked Damon hard at the back of the head. He dropped like a stone. Other jocks were slow to react, as Annaliese kicked and double punched for all she was worth, creating distraction and chaos as others fell or backed away.

April reacted instinctively, yanking her pelvis up and crushing Shirl in a headlock, she maneuvered wrestling style to overpower her opponent. Another jock fell nearby to Annaliese's blows. He had been in the process of pulling a knife. April grabbed the blade with both hands tied, twisted her thighs violently, and sprang free.

In a state of undress, the girls stood together, facing the three remaining jocks still standing. Davy threw a punch at one of them; he was not a fighter, but was doing his best. April whispered aside, "Free your hands on this knife, then free me. Let's take these assholes together. Go girl!"

The girls leapt to the offensive, the jocks not ready, and too drunk to counter the initial strikes. However, they regrouped as the others reanimated and set to a maul, restricting the girls' movements and slowly closing them down.

Cornered, Damon grabbed Shirl's knife and advanced threateningly. Annaliese backed away, and April wanted to do likewise, but she knew she had to take him out, once and for all. She spat with derision, "I'm gonna make sure you never try to rape another innocent girl again, pond scum."

She spat and Damon slowed, keeping just out of range of her lethal kicks. April teased him, "Not such a big man now Huh! Afraid of a girl who fights back. All bully's are in fact cowards, aren't you Damon."

Chapter 16

Damon took a small, belligerent step forwards, and that was all April needed. She somersaulted backwards, but her body moved forwards through the air. Her left foot kicked the knife out of his hand, her right heel driving up beneath his jaw. The force was so violent his skull flipped back; something cracked.

Annaliese was already taking on another attacker, when Davy shouted, "I ain't no rapist," and kicked the jock attacking Annaliese between his legs. He dropped to the floor, clutching his jewels and cursing.

The two remaining jocks were soon overpowered, each receiving a kick to the chin to ensure their unconsciousness. They were a mess, and looked like they had spent too long in the ring with Mike Tyson.

The Davy backed away, "Sorry girls. Damon told us you were up for some fun, so I came along to join the party. I never knew this shit was going down. You OK? Here, I'm Davy, cover yourself with my jacket. This ain't no way to treat a lady. Shit man! I've had it messin' with these dudes."

Movement behind the man's shoulder caught April's attention; "Get the bitch. Don't let her escape—she filmed it."

Davy grabbed Shirl as she made the top of the stairs, and brought back to face April. "Hand over your cell, bitch."

The girl smiled in an odd sort of way, and handed April a cell phone from her bag. April punched her hard in the stomach, "Now hand over the other cell, the one you used to video us."

The smile disappeared as the girl fumbled in her bag, her eyes darting around. April smashed her forcefully, full in the mouth, teeth flying everywhere.

"I guess she'll be eating through a straw in future."

Annaliese quipped, "Get her cell, get all the others, this is going nowhere."

Annaliese's eyes bored into April's; she was preventing any fallout. April realized what was at stake if word made it onto campus, and nodded her head.

The cache of cell phones safe, the girls changed into their regular clothes with as much modesty as possible, and packed up their stuff. Davy had Shirl under close scrutiny. She was crying as she searched for her missing teeth, there were quite a few of them.

When they were dressed, April said to the turncoat, "Here's your jacket back, thanks. Nothing happened here, understand?"

She moved to stand menacingly over Shirl. The girl backed
away and reached into her purse, pulling out a roll, "Here, take it.
It's all the money I have. Please don't hurt me."

April leaned over oppressively and spat, "I don't need your
money, bi-otch. I need you, and these numbskulls gone from my
life. Understand! Next time I will kill you."

Shirl shrank back, and fled for the stairs. Davy shuffled away,
"OK." He held out his palms, as if asking for calm, "This is
between you and them. It stays between you and them, OK. You
two living rough here? You can surf my sofa if you want?"

Before April could reply, Annaliese said, "Thanks, but no
thanks. We were only messin' here. Come-on April, time we
headed home."

They started walking at once. Davy called out, "At least let me
give you a lift."

The girls ignored him, they were pissed, emotions a whirl of
conflict: Scared one moment, brave the next. Almost victims,
almost killers. What they were not was calm, they were
traumatized.

They talked in staccato bursts, followed by silences. The
threat, the wounds to themselves, their egos still too raw for
nurture. Their hearts too pained to remember all. They were on
edge until they cleared the campus gate. April spoke into the night,
"So 'Miss-know-it-all', where're we headed for?"

Annaliese replied, "I've zero ideas. I just wanted to get the hell
out of there, and I wasn't going to jump from any frying pan into a
fire. Got us out the school gate. What you got in mind?"

"Woah there!" said a voice from the darkness behind. They
turned as campus security came over, "The late bus stops over
there, see, just passed those trash cans. Heah, you two OK?"

April replied, "Never felt better, but it's been a long day.
Thanks, when's the bus due?"

They were quiet, not wishing to speak, even though the late
bus was almost empty. It was personal and private. Annaliese was
lost in her thoughts, memories of other events resurfacing, when
April grabbed her hand as she bolted for the door.

Annaliese watched the bus depart, and looked around. They
appeared to be in the middle of nowhere, all she saw was the river
and some boats, the bright lights of civilization twinkled in the

Chapter 16

distance. Nearby was a sign for a marina and moorings. She said, "This is your plan? I ain't dossin' down here. Where is this place? Looks like the end of the world to me."

April replied with aplomb, "This is the beginning of a new adventure. We need to put the past behind us tonight, and tomorrow will happen to us whenever it does. Let's try the store."

They entered a place that was larger than Rosa's, and although similar, sold an odd assortment of camping and boat related stuff. Annaliese lugged a carrier basket around, while April filled it with frozen pizza, and whatever took her fancy. She topped off with chilled beers, a bottle of Italian red, and another of Rebel Yell. "Get some snacks and whatever you fancy Liese, here's the cash. I need to go check something."

Annaliese arrived back with several carriers, and found her friend studying the information wall. April was taking snapshots, but noting her friends arrival said, "Do you fancy Mr. Sea Ray Sundancer's place tonight, or Mr. Beneteau's Blue II?"

April took her last camera shot, and split the bags, the weight with Annaliese. She headed off, Annaliese trying to make any sense of her intentions. They snuck into the marina through the fence, avoiding security, and April stopped to survey the boardwalks and gangplanks.

"Mr. Sundancer has security out back. Shame, that boat is for sale at over one mill, Hon. Mr. Beneteau looks empty, but the neighbors will spot us for sure. Wait a minute. Look over there, way out back.

They found a towpath and squeezed through the fence, onto public land. "That looks like a floating home, no neighbors, cool. Hello Mr. Funco. Come-on Liese, break in while I get the power and water on."

Sometime later the girls were relaxing in the saloon. "This is what I call living rough Liese. Cheers!" They touched beer bottles and drank. The microwave pinged, their pizza was ready. "I'll get that," April announced, "You get some more beers out the fridge."

Later they got blitzed on Rebel Yell, their recent trauma was still too fresh a wound for healing. A couple of days passed them by in ignorant bliss of any world outside. When they shared, talk turned to what almost happened to them, it was not full cleansing, but good therapy all the same.

"How can you be like this? We were almost raped for Christ's sakes! If you had not taken that jock out, he would have raped me, there was zero … and I mean nothing I could do about it."

Annaliese stroked April's hair and whispered encouragingly, "Maybe, Hon. The fact is you saved me from being raped. I simply returned the favor. It ain't no big deal, as long as nothing happens of course. Nothing happened, OK."

April shook her head, "No, that's not it. For the very first time since I ran away from home, I felt vulnerable. I need time to deal with this. Tell me, how did you survive, like inside, all those conflicting emotions, and all that crap head stuff?"

Talking helped them both, and they cheered as the day went on. Feeling more like their old selves, they made a pact to finish the incident, and get on with their lives. As a show of conviction, they took all the cell phones, turned them on, and threw them as far as they could into the river.

After a less drunken, and more fulfilling evening, they were hauling themselves out of the abyss. Talk turned to college and Kung Fu, a sure sign they were getting their shit together. The cause of their recent trauma reappeared, they still had not found anywhere to live. The boat would have to do for the time being.

Later that morning they froze, voices were approaching; "Yeah, had her in the family for a long time. I don't really want to sell her, but the kids have flown the coop, and what with the wife wanting to move nearer her invalid mother, well, you understand."

The buyer patted the hull and said, "OK if I take a look inside? She's just what we are looking for."

The apparent owner made a cell call, "My wife is coming with the keys, but she wants to tidy up first; check everything is OK. She won't be long. Why don't I show you the mooring office and dry-dock, boats need to have their hulls cleaned once a year…"

The voices faded away, the girls looked at each other and without needing words, packed their stuff. Once clear, Annaliese said, "That was a close. You got any more 'bright ideas', April?"

Her friend replied without hesitation, "Yeah. I'd die for just one night on that Sundancer. That was fun though, admit it Liese."

Determined to get on with their lives, they returned to college. Butcho-jock Damon was being pushed around campus in a wheelchair by Shirl, he had on a neck support, and their peers were shunning them. Annaliese was expecting taunts and jibes, but it seemed nothing had been said.

April was surprised, and feared the worst when admin called for her. She had no idea what was going on. Upon proof of ID she was handed a brown cardboard box, it was marked interstate, Seattle. She found a private place, removed the burner cell from the package, and called the only number in the memory.

"Hon, you OK? I tried calling… The thing is, your mother was released from prison, but only to a mental remission unit. She'd be on their main program, except she is female. Seems she got some dumb-schmuck story past the authorities. They believed she was only assisting Rupert because of something related to Stockholm's Syndrome. I don't believe shit, but she is now at…"

April's world fell apart. She left bureaucracy behind her, unsure of how she felt. Annaliese found her under the Big Oak, people crowding around, but she was on her own. "Care to share?"

April offered Annaliese her brown paper carrier, and took a sip from the Rebel Yell hidden inside, before handing it back. "This ain't no way to go Hon, what happened?"

April took another slug before replying, "They let her out. I just found out. How could they?"

"Your mom?"

April's almost pleading eyes locked with Annaliese's. Abstractly April added, "They got her in some psycho rehab unit for women up near Jericho. You got a trumpet? Those walls are coming down. She is under the quack, but otherwise she is out free. I intend to kill her for what she almost did to me."

Annaliese cared for her friend, eventually deciding it was better to let her get trashed, and begin again in the morning. She knew things usually looked a lot brighter the next day, or whenever the trauma passed. They spent the night in a derelict factory, not that April knew much about it. Annaliese watched over her like a guardian angle and kept her friend safe.

The next day was different, but not in any way Annaliese expected; "I have to face her, shoot her down. Mother may have hoodwinked everybody else, but I do not believe a word of her lies. Let's head for the library, I need to research this real good."

Chapter 17 – Payback

"April, give me the pistol. You don't need a gun to go see your mother."

"Hmmm. Maybe I do," April nonchalantly replied, sliding a bullet directly into the barrel, and replacing the slider. "I need to end this for all time."

"So you think that by shoving an extra bullet up the barrel, that will somehow make everything all right. I love you, but sometimes Hon, you are quite stupid. When you get mad you get tunnel-vision. Here, give it to me."

April replied with half-assed sexual innuendo, "Is that a threat or a promise, sweetheart." She pouted a dismissive kiss in Annaliese's direction.

Unprepared for the attack, April was on her back before she knew what hit her. Annaliese insistent, lying on top of her and pinning her down. "Give me the gun!"

Annaliese knew that April's thoughts were misaligned, her feelings of wonton revenge dwarfing her normal equilibrium. "Give it up April or I promise, I will never kiss you, ever again."

April stuck out her tongue, which Annaliese fastened her lips around, and began to suck, hard. April thought she was making out, until the suction got so bad it hurt. It got worse. April gave up the pistol and flapped her arms around in submission.

Annaliese let go of her prey, stashing the gun safely away. "You got one hell of a suck girl!" April admonished.

Annaliese looked awry, "You ain't the only one haunted by demons, Hon. Had to learn how to do that real good for those fine and upstanding, god-fearing menfolk up there in 'Arid-Zona'..."

She could not complete her reiteration of remembered subjugation. April smothered her with love. It was no longer sex. Somehow, they had moved on, deeper into true intimacy, and knowledge of one another. They loved one another in other ways, both sharing a deeper understanding of what it meant to be 'a woman' in contemporary society.

The following day, Annaliese helped April search the web, and she found April's mother, her schedule, and began to piece together a plan. April slowly came on board. "No guns, no kung fu, OK. Your only weapons are words. You got that April?"

Chapter 17

April replied, distracted, "Sure. Got that, you're right. I'm goin' to decimate the bitch though, watch me."

April stood and got her stuff, but turned to look back, just before she opened the door. "I can't progress as a person in my own right, until I put all this shit behind me. I have to face her, call her out, or otherwise I am nothing. This is going to be the hardest thing I have ever done in my life."

§

Sally Waverly

"Sally Waverley?"

The voice was one the woman knew, but could not place. It sounded vaguely familiar. She turned her head to see who it was, and didn't recognize the speaker.

The person took a photograph of her and put the cell back inside her top shirt pocket; she did not realize it was voice recording. The stranger squatted down beside her, and looked menacingly into her eyes. Sally was instantly afraid for her life.

"Mother, you and I are going to take a little walk, there are some matters from way back when we need to discuss. Don't make any fuss now, or I will kill you; right here, right now."

Sally was dragged forcefully to her feet, and ushered away by her daughter. "Please don't hurt me, it was all Rupert's doing—his idea to sell you, his contacts, I just went along with his plan."

"No you did not mother. It was your idea, your contacts. He was scared of his own shadow. I heard you on the landline, why do you think I ran for my life? Huh!"

"But I…"

"No you did not mother. You told Rupert to get the wine so you could celebrate selling my virginity. I was thirteen years old! I was still a child for God's sakes! So help me God, but I want to kill you so bad. What you did was unforgivable."

"But it didn't happen Shona, you escaped. I've been so worried about you."

"Don't change the subject. Don't pretend, you cared. Mother, you did not care or give a shit about me. It's time you were honest with yourself, bitch."

They took a bench near the river, where they would be alone and could see anyone approach. It was just along from the dumpster, which was why April chose it.

Sally's hands fidgeted as if they had a mind of their own. Her eyes darted about, as if searching for phantoms, but never focusing on anything for long.

April put an arm around her shoulder, and gripped her with force, pulling her closer. "It's like this 'Sweetie'," April's eyes bored menacingly into her mother's. "Your only chance of living is to tell me why. Everything."

Sally quailed, she did not want to revisit her early years, they were all too painful, the scars still fresh in her mind. She swallowed hard when the voice beside her spoke, "I know you were a hooker, into the pants and wallets of any man in uniform. Was it just for money, or did you get off on it? How did you hoodwink my Dad?"

Sally's shoulders slumped, the moment she had been dreading all her life had finally arrived. She knew this time there was no escape. She truly loved her daughter, missed her; she still wanted to be her mother. Her eyes watered and she held her head up, letting the tears roll down her cheeks unchecked.

"Start at the very beginning, mother. I want to hear it all from your own lips."

Sally had nowhere to run, her eyes became focused on somewhere far off within the uttermost reaches of time. The words when they came were measured, as if she were reading aloud the story of her younger self from an auto-que.

"I can't remember my own mother. I know I had one, and sometimes I think I feel her watching over me, but there is nothing in my memory. She is a ghost to me.

"I do remember having another mother, but she was a hippy. Later I found out she adopted me when I was a toddler. I never managed to put that behind me, being rejected by my birth parents. My father, my adoptive one, was never there. He flew planes for the Air Force, fighters, and was often away on military service. I never could settle in any school, as we moved around a lot, so I was home-schooled. My mother was usually off her head, and had many friends around, mainly men friends.

"My father treated me real swell, the few times he was there. He used to take me into the base to watch the planes take off and land. He even swung it so I sat in the pilot's seat of his jet one time. He also took me into the Officer's Mess, and I was the star of all his buddies, they always gave me a great welcome. That was one of the last … the few times I can ever remember being happy."

"That's ancient history, Mother, and has nothing to do with how you treated me." April admonished, trying to hurry the story along.

For the first time Sally looked at her and said, "I thought you wanted to hear it all. That's why I got this thing about men in uniform. I automatically trusted them, plus they had a steady job and good money.

"Now where was I? Oh yes. There was some sort of war thing going on, Vietnam I guess. Anyway, he got shot down and arrived back in the U.S. in a body bag. My mother never got her head straight enough to make the service with full honors. Some of his buddies collected me, and looked after me through the funeral. I was given the Flag. I wanted my father's arms to hold me, just one more time. Instead, I held a wrap of colored cotton. It wasn't a fair exchange. I still have it.

"After that, mother moved to Frisco, and we hung out with some of her old pals. I was becoming a tweenie. Don't ask me dates or my age, because I don't know. In those days it was all weed, resin, H, uppers and downers. You will have new names for them nowadays. Mostly we did LSD … I still have flashbacks. Shona, know that if I am still alive when you leave, then I am bound to have one tonight. But that isn't important to you, is it.

"It was around that time I lost my virginity. I don't know who to, or even remember anything at all about it. Mother made money and got drugs, food sometimes, and alcohol … by then she was turning tricks, and taught me to do the same. It was the only life I knew until she OD'd one day, and I was left to fend for myself. I did the only thing I knew, offered my body in exchange for any means to survive.

"I ended up in a real school when I was thirteen going on fourteen. Uncle Bernie rescued me after the bailiff's came knocking for rent arrears, and he stuck a plaster over the ruins my life had become.

"I was put in foster care, but although they tried, I did not adapt well. I continued my old life around my new one. At fifteen we had a break in Vegas, and I loved the place. My foster parents were on the machines and shooting craps, and I let them get on with it. I had my freedom, and was shooting up crap I bought out on the streets. To pay for it, other men shot their crap into me. I made a lot of money. I did what I needed to do to survive."

Her mother turned to look at her, but April was quiet, absorbed. Obviously, this was not what she had expected to hear. Sally relaxed slightly and continued, "I did more or less the same thing for years afterwards. Different places, different Johns, but the essence of my life never changed much.

"Through a friend I met on the streets, I got invited to go with her to some military functions. I already told you I have a thing about men in uniform, and why. At first, I was there just to make up the numbers, but I worked my angle, and became a regular 'party girl', as they called us. We was hookers, Hon. I'm not proud of it, and yet I am. I was good at what I did."

April roused, angry and confrontational, "So why did you latch onto Dad?"

Sally sighed wistfully; she knew this was it. "There was always something special about your father, Shona. He partied harder than most, but was deeper, and also not a 'Yessir' man. He had his own mind, one I respected. In the strangest of ways, he reminded me of my mother.

"The other thing was, I had some other shit going down at that time, and needed to escape. Your father, for all his physical strength and worldly wisdom, was an easy catch for me."

April reared and spat, "So you married him to save your own butt, and get an easy life. Don't tell me, I know already. You weren't running around on him, you were back on the game. Jesus Christ mother, I cannot believe you!"

Sally's tears began to fall once more, she mumbled, "It wasn't like that, but I guess you are right. I loved your father you know. I wanted it to work out with him and tried my best, but my past caught up with me. Remember that Shona, the past always catches up with you. No matter how cleaver you think you are at hiding it; just like us here now.

"I went to the store. I needed a test kit. I thought I might be carrying your brother, but it turned out I was not. I had turned my life around, the old one long gone. That was until I saw Leverndale, and I ran for my car. He was one of the worst I had worked for. A mobster, ex-pimp, and extremely cruel with it.

Chapter 17

"I got home free, but he must have followed me, tracked me down somehow. He was waiting for me as I parked the car one day, and insisted we talk inside. He had stuff on me, stuff I knew your father could never accept. Mostly it was sex, but not all of it.

"Shona, the thing was, he didn't want me ... he wanted you!"

April's eyes flashed sideways, flicking fixated on her mother's, this was not something she had expected. Sally knew she had just ripped her daughter's known world apart, but she had asked for it. Wanting rid of it all, she finished the story.

"What was I to do? I offered myself to keep you safe. Most of it wasn't normal sex either. Your dad caught me out, and I admitted having a fling, then a lover, I wanted to protect him from that bozo. I wanted to keep us together as a family, but it was not to be.

"Leverndale was a control freak, and as nasty as they come. I did not leave Bill because I didn't love you both, I left to keep you safe. Leverndale promised that if I lived alone, did everything he asked of me, he would lay off you. That's the God's honest truth. I hid what I did from you, but you almost found out. I had to leave, we made a run for it, or don't you remember? I thought we were clear, but that guy we lived with was a total jerk.

"I was looking for a way out, a new place for us to live, when Leverndale found me again. He told me his minder would live with me—that was Rupert. He was a pedophile, and he was not harmless. He was there to report back on you. So yes, when I said Rupert was the instigator, in many ways he was. That was his job, to report back to his boss. I protected you from him getting his jollies, OK."

April stood up and looked all around, before saying, "This sucks. If I ever discover, just one word of what you have told me is a lie, I will come back and put a bullet through your brain. Just like I did Rupert."

Sally smiled for the first time and replied, "Well done. I hoped somebody would kill that good for nothing. Chip off the old block after all, eh?"

April turned to face her mother down, she was pissed again, "Finish this mother, I need you, and all your personal history gone from my life."

Sally's brief moment of happiness turned sour. She had hoped her daughter would become a part of her life, either that or end it.

126

Death would have been a great release. Instead, Sally stared vacantly at nothing, as she gathered her words. "There's little more to tell.

"Otis, Leverndale always wanted you as his personal whore, and I guess I was only keeping him at bay for a while. Rupert was into young girls, ones your age back then. He was Leverndale's ears and eyes, and had eyes on some of your school friends also. That's why I stopped them coming round. You thought I had it in for you. That's not true, I knew what was really going down."

"Bullshit Mother. If he were Leverndale's creature, he would not have been trying to get into my pants all those times. Times, I'll remind you Mother, you turned a blind eye to. Until there was money on the table.

"You forget, I heard the glee in your voice when you were on the phone. You may have been scared that Rupert would 'damage the goods' but you were wonton for the money, and you didn't give a shit what happened to me!"

Sally quavered, "They ... these people are sick, but I endured it all, and ended up the way I am. That ain't no excuse, it's just the way my life panned out. You don't want to know what they forced me to do after you ran away ... I have never felt so intimately or utterly violated in all my life. Jail was a sanctuary compared to that..."

April

April saw her mother's eyes drift far away, outwards her focus, inwards her vision. In that moment, she realized that sometimes it was better not to know the whole truth. She squeezed her mother's shoulder in passing, and made her way out via the stream.

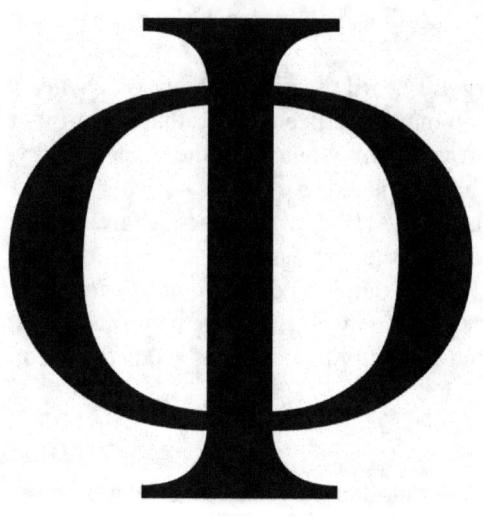

Chapter 18 – A Bright New Tomorrow

"How'd it go," Annaliese asked when her friend returned later that morning. They were in a café near the main LA bus station.

"Mother is still alive, if that's what you wanted to know. I guess she had it worse than either of us. But she still wanted me to live out the same wreck of a life she had lived."

Annaliese came close to comfort her, but April shied away, turning to face her friend. "There is one man I will execute. A gangsta I saw from a doorway, the night when he came by to claim my virginity. I now know his name. Otis Leverndale, and he is a dead man walking."

They left immediately for the nearest library, finding an out of the way desk with a few computers. The hits came immediately, "Gangland turf war," "Sex warehouse raided," "Father kills pedophile hoodlum." The headlines did not give much detail, and it took them forty minutes and searches of police and court press releases before they unraveled the case.

"Look here," Annaliese enthused as she read the article. "A father had seen his twelve year old daughter being abducted by the hoods, and he followed them. He called 911, before going to save her. There was a firefight, and the leader, Otis Leverndale was shot in the heart. The father also took gunshot wounds, but lived, only to be locked up for murder. The police killed many with impunity. The daughter, along with thirty other girls of mixed ages, were rescued. This newspaper demands the father be set free."

"I gotta do something Liese, this is so unfair. I have to find the girl, the family." It wasn't easy, but they got the father's name, Samuel J. Waterman. From this they were able to trace the mother and children.

April wanted to go and see them, but Liese protested, "This is madness. They will not want reminding of the past, would you? If you must ease your conscience, make a donation to the Save Samuel J Waterman Fund." And that is what April did.

That afternoon a small, dizzy blonde emerged from an abandoned building, and walked purposefully towards a cemetery. She found the grave of Otis Leverndale; the citation read 'Rest in Peace'. Ensuring no one was watching, she took out her

Chapter 18

Leatherman and plunged it into a grave repeatedly. Over the headstone she sprayed the word 'PEDO', and immediately made tracks.

April removed her disguise before they got the hell out of LA. Once back on campus, April switched her cell back on and said, "I feel real good about today, but we still got nowhere to live, any ideas?"

Annaliese said, "Good food and a proper bed it shall be, anything else you want?"

"Yeah, I want to be surrounded by normal people for a while, what you got?"

Annaliese grinned and returned a call. Intrigued, April rounded on her, but Annaliese kept turning away and whispering until she put the cell down. "C'mon Liese! Give it up."

Annaliese said, "Better grab your stuff, Manny will be outside the main gate in a minute. Today is Rosa's birthday, and they are celebrating. You know what that means…"

The girls raced outside. Teves waiting, his arms opened wide in greeting as they rushed to him, their sometimes surrogate father.

He was entertaining on the short journey, and dropped them off outside a ramshackle hotel in the middle of nowhere, somewhat east of San Diego. They knew the place well.

Marisol was stoking an oil-drum barbeque on what was planned to be the saloon terrace, but hadn't got it going properly. Teves immediately took over, teasing the charcoal with experienced hands, eyes, and puffs of breath.

On seeing the girls, Marisol let out a whoop of joy and ran to them. Moments later, Rosa encircled all of them in her motherly arms, before kissing them in turn. Breaking away she issued a string of instructions; she was distracting them, keeping everybody focused on the here and now, and the joys of life.

Later, April and Annaliese enjoyed a cold beer and the unmistakable taste of freedom. Xochitl, Teves' wife came over, her hands hidden behind her back. "Buenas noches. Welcome home. I know but little, Chiquitas. I cannot imagine. I have Manny cooking burgers and chicken for you, he is excellent with BBQ. He will not be happy unless you share with him—here."

Xochitl produced a bottle of liquor, saying, "I do not approve of this, normally, but tonight is a rare exception. This is the finest Tequila from my parent's village, my cousin made it himself. It has the power to make you remember, or to forget. If you have no memory, then the future seems bright. You need to see the future, not what has passed already. Lay the ghosts that haunt you this night, and live again a bright new life with the morning sun. Our Good Lord has more work for you to do, I know it."

Neither girl could remember much the next morning, heads throbbed, but the past had miraculously faded away. As they reanimated to face the day, Annaliese pulled back the drapes. The sun shone brightly, not a cloud in the sky.

Annaliese cursed as April shielded her eyes from the sunlight. She closed the drapes and said, "It sure is bright out there, Hon. I guess this is our bright new tomorrow, where's my shades?"

After a hearty breakfast, and fond farewells, Teves insisted on giving them a ride back to college. It was the last thing either needed or wanted, but they did their day, and survived. Come sundown, they had studied well, but still had nowhere to live.

The girls stayed the next two nights in a derelict factory, followed by three more surfing sofa's in a student squat. Their grades and Kung Fu skills were slipping, and April knew it. They just wanted to survive.

One of the clique gave them a tip, which was a dud. Sure, the place had beds available, but not the type of share they were expecting. Disillusioned, they headed off into the night hauling heavy holdalls. April stopped at the store and they bought some snacks and juice. Annaliese was getting wrung-out keeping April sane.

There was a local information wall and they looked at it, but most were sales ads. Annaliese spotted one that was old, and difficult to read. She got the street name, "Sacramento Drive," but could not make out the number, faded over time. The ad read, "Live-in help required. Michael."

April snapped the address with her cell and getting directions from the staff, walked smartly away. She said over her shoulder, "We have to discover our destiny. I'm fed up with living in the past and present. C'mon Liese, this is new, the future could be exiting."

The girls walked for ages until they finally found the road. Their feet hurt and they were way past tired. Annaliese quipped, piqued with frustration, "I'm pissed. There's gotta be a room for rent somewhere in Aztec. We've been walking forever. Zilch!"

Chapter 18

She threw her bag down on the sidewalk and slumped her butt on the curb. "I suppose we could commute from Rosa's. But without transport, or even with, it's a long chunk out of each day."

April humored her best friend, "Here, have some of my isotonic juice, it'll help keep you going. That ad on the info-wall said there was a place down this road, we just gotta find it, Hon."

They sat in silence, their thoughts lost within the drudgery of trudgery. April had been staring at the house for … she didn't know how long. There was a sign in the window she couldn't read from so far away. It seemed to call to her. She was drawn to it, walked towards it, and found a scribbled note in joined-up writing. It was almost illegible until she was very close. It read, "HELP WANTED. Apply within. Michael."

April drew her fingernails across the sign from the other side of the grimy glass pane, knowing they had found their destiny; intuitively, she rang the bell…

The End

Fractured Book Two: Conspiracy Theory

Continues the adventures of April and Annaliese, as they save the U.S. from nuclear devastation. Enter Michael, who warps this intrigue into another dimension of inter-agency, and intra-governmental conspiracy.

Conspiracy Theory combines mystery, thriller, espionage, and terrorist threat in one breathtaking novel. Masterminded by the head of a global conglomerate, to destroy governance and the American way of life; the premise so simple to accomplish.

Could it happen in real life, today? Certainly.

Can April and Annaliese thwart the ambitions of a megalomaniac?

About the Author

John C. Morris [Jonno], has never accepted anything because it is the accepted 'norm'. "Why?" is what he asks by return? "Whose 'norm?' Not mine, I am sure.

"What of your life—the one you are living right now. What do **you** believe in?"

Morris admits, "I have enjoyed so many different careers, and seen so much of the world in the process, they seem like separate lifetimes.

"I always wanted to be a folk/rock star, because I have always been driven to tell stories of peoples lives and loves, by writing lyrics. Whilst being very good at playing a 12-string acoustic guitar, I could not sing to save my life. Over time, I discovered I could write, teenage rebellion songs, poems and short stories first, and later novels."

Born in England and living in China since 2004, Morris has held numerous positions, from the ten years he spent as a police officer specializing in serious fraud, to entrepreneur and world trader, to writer. Early on, he qualified as Yachtmaster for sailing vessels.

Married to a supportive (and long-suffering) Cantonese wife, their young daughter is now the light of his life, abstractly named, 'Rhiannon'.

"Cantonese cannot pronounce the letter 'R'", he cast aside glibly. "So her full name is 'Rhiannon Dorothea Morris'. You gotta love all those 'rrr' sounds. Heah! I am bad."

Although he and his wife do not share a common language, they communicate exceptionally well. Morris writes about his cross-cultural experiences on his web site, www.china-expats.com.

Morris draws on his eclectic life experiences on his author website www.john-morris-author.com/.